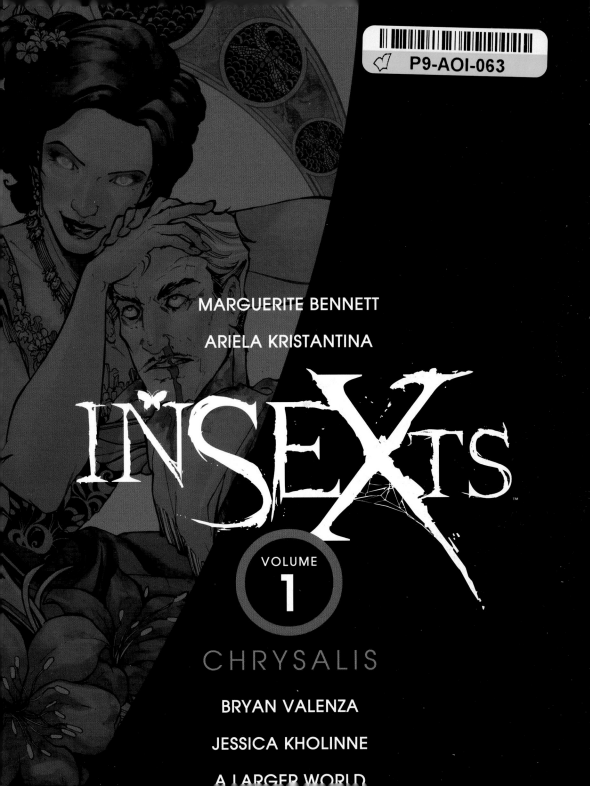

MARGUERITE BENNETT

ARIELA KRISTANTINA

INSEXts

VOLUME
1

CHRYSALIS

BRYAN VALENZA

JESSICA KHOLINNE

A LARGER WORLD

IN

SEXTS

VOLUME 1

CHRYSALIS

MARGUERITE BENNETT creator & writer

ARIELA KRISTANTINA artist

BRYAN VALENZA (#1-5) & **JESSICA KHOLINNE** (#6-7) colorists

A LARGER WORLD'S TROY PETERI letterer

ARIELA KRISTANTINA w/ **BRYAN VALENZA** front cover

ARIELA KRISTANTINA w/ **BRYAN VALENZA** original series covers

JOHN CASSADAY w/ **PAUL MOUNTS** &
PHIL HESTER variant covers

JOHN J. HILL book & logo designer

MIKE MARTS editor

AFTERSHOCK™

MIKE MARTS - Editor-in-Chief • **JOE PRUETT** - Publisher • **LEE KRAMER** - President
JAWAD QURESHI - SVP, Investor Relations • **JON KRAMER** - Chief Executive Officer
MIKE ZAGARI - SVP Digital/Creative • **JAY BEHLING** - CFO • **MICHAEL RICHTER** - Chief Creative Officer
STEPHAN NILSON - Publishing Operations Coordinator • **LISA Y. WU** - Social Media Coordinator

AfterShock Trade Dress and Interior Design by **JOHN J. HILL**
AfterShock Logo Design by **COMICRAFT**
Proofreading by **J. HARBORE** & **DOCTOR Z.**
Publicity: contact **AARON MARION** (aaron@fifteenminutes.com) &
RYAN CROY (ryan@fifteenminutes.com) at **15 MINUTES**

AFTERSHOCKCOMICS.COM Follow us on social media 🐦 📷 f

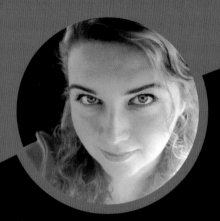

INTRODUCTION

"Erotic Body Horror?"

Now why would a nice girl from a nice family want to write something like that?

I wrote InSEXts because I am a woman, and to be a woman is to live a life of body horror.

If you are female, you learn early that something is wrong with you, and that you will be punished for it. You are told you are weaker than others. You are told to be dainty. You are told to be modest, sweet, smiling, quiet…your body is trained. Your body is restrained. You know that to be female is to be flawed. You know it is degrading to be a girl, to be likened to a girl. *You hit like a girl. You cry like a pussy. You whine like a little bitch. You're not like other girls.*

As you grow and age, your body distorts. It grows curves and distensions; it swells and aches; it cramps and bleeds. You will be treated differently. Authorities will make you cover your body. You will be sent home if your body is not covered enough. Your classmates cannot be expected to behave with respect or control—your body is to blame. Strangers make comments about your body. Strangers follow you because of your body. They express their desire to do things to your body. They may hurt your body because of their ability or inability to do the things they desire. They may hurt your body because of what they do or not find there.

Your body is an untrustworthy ally, a traitor in waiting. You grow hair on your body, which you are told is dirty and disgusting, and which you cut off or rip out, but it always returns. You sweat. There are scents to your body that are not fruity or floral. You scrub and clean and cut and bleach and paint and highlight and condition and spray and fast and tan and train and powder and contour and starve but nothing is ever enough to perfect the expectations on your body. You are criticized for needing or even for wanting to do these things, though you are punished when you fail to do them. But even if you achieve the correct image without these actions, you will be despised for aging and the fading of the beauty of your body. Your youth is valued, your desirability, your sexual availability, and these things are fleeting and determined by strangers.

Your body will hurt you sometimes—organs shifting, changing, growing, expelling. You may be capable of having children. A partner may revile you for being unable to have children. A partner may revile you for being with child at an undesired time. The having or not having of children is your fault and blame. Your body is not your own. Your body belongs to others. You will be punished for your body, with your body.

And because of this, I wrote a story about all the horror and power and sensuality and rage of the bodies of women, metamorphic. What is soft becomes hard; what is gentle becomes sharp. Clicking teeth and chittering mandibles live under warm flesh. What was colonized and enslaved breaks free.

Why would I write this?

I am a woman. I live in a world of body horror.

And so do you.

MARGUERITE BENNETT
August 3, 2016
Los Angeles

1
"CHRYSALIS"

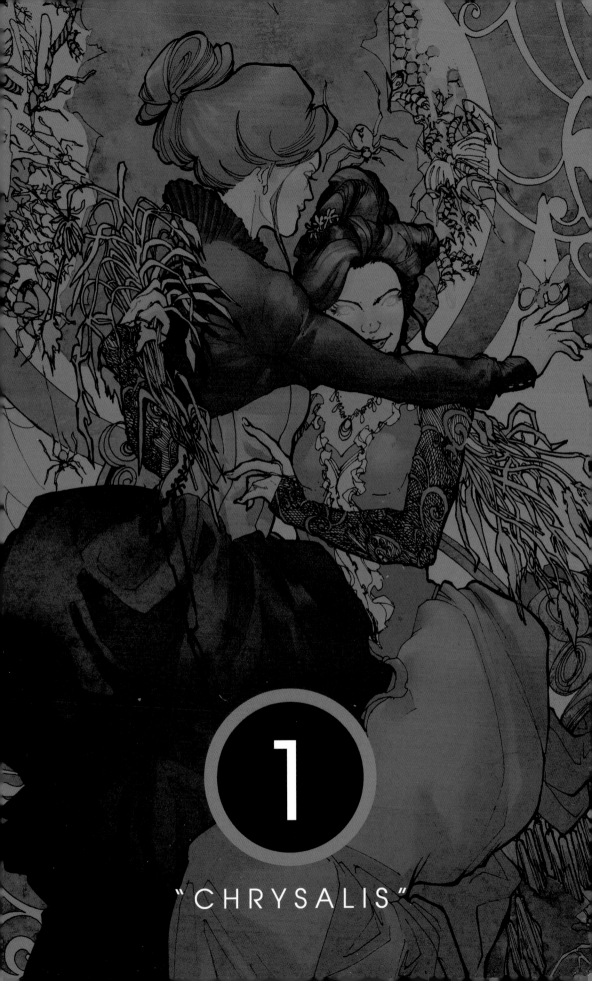

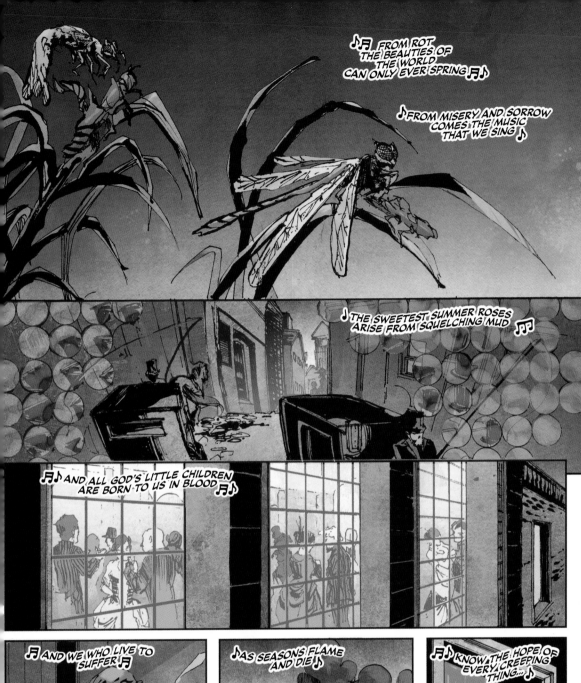

♪♫ FROM ROT THE BEAUTIES OF THE WORLD CAN ONLY EVER SPRING ♫♪

♪ FROM MISERY AND SORROW COMES THE MUSIC THAT WE SING ♪

♪ THE SWEETEST SUMMER ROSES ARISE FROM SQUELCHING MUD ♫♪

♫♪ AND, ALL GOD'S LITTLE CHILDREN ARE BORN TO US IN BLOOD ♫♪

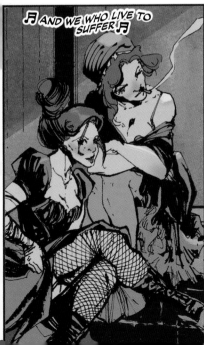

♫ AND WE WHO LIVE TO SUFFER ♫

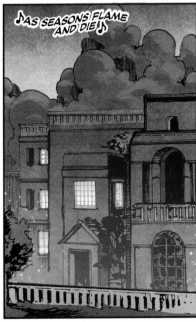

♪ AS SEASONS FLAME AND DIE ♪

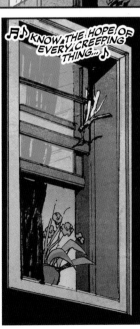

♫♪ KNOW THE HOPE OF EVERY CREEPING THING... ♪

♪♬ ...TO BE A BUTTERFLY ♬♪
EUH!
SQLCH

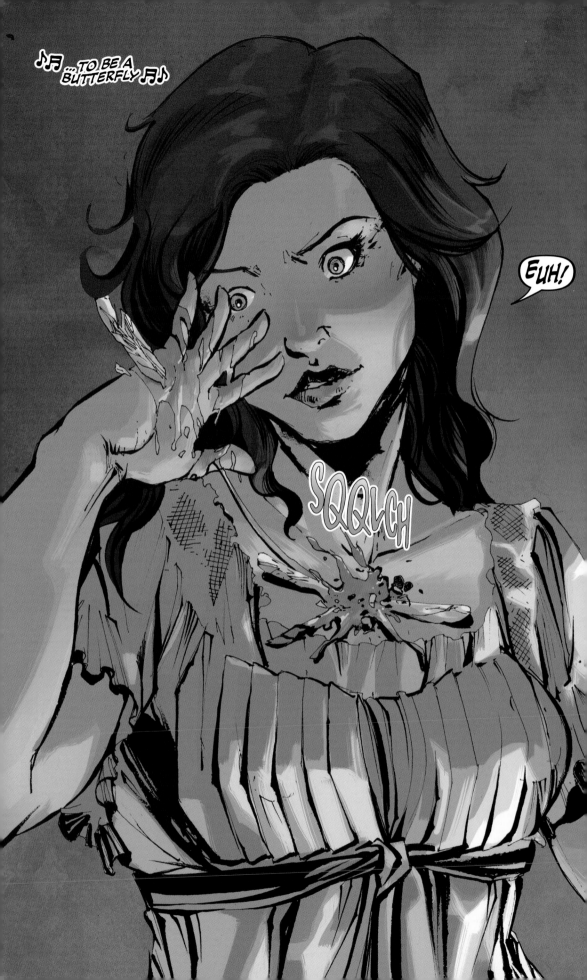

London 1894
!
DID IT STING YOU, MY LADY?
OH, MARIAH--
HERE, YOU ARE BLEEDING--
MARIAH, DON'T. DON'T...
HOW CAN YOU BE CONCERNED WITH SO SLIGHT A THING--WITH ME?!
AFTER... AFTER WHAT MY HUSBAND HAS DONE?

DID HE HURT YOU, MARIAH?
NO, MY LADY.
NOT BADLY.
I CAN'T LET YOU BE HARMED LIKE THIS!
I-I CAN SEND YOU AWAY, IF YOU LIKE. MY SISTER IS IN AMERICA. I CAN SEND YOU TO HER--
I WOULD NOT BE PARTED FROM YOU, MY LADY.

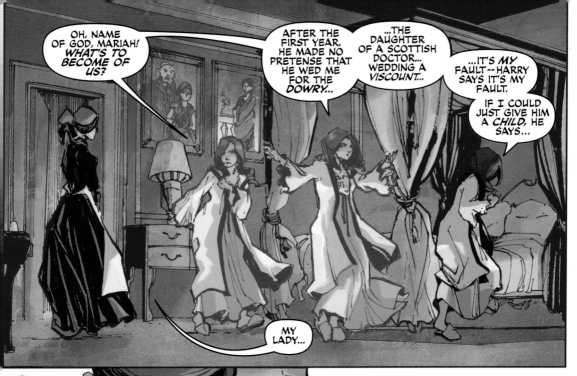

OH, NAME OF GOD, MARIAH! *WHAT'S TO BECOME OF US?*

AFTER THE FIRST YEAR, HE MADE NO PRETENSE THAT HE WED ME FOR THE *DOWRY...*

...THE DAUGHTER OF A SCOTTISH DOCTOR... WEDDING A *VISCOUNT...*

...IT'S *MY FAULT* -- HARRY SAYS IT'S MY FAULT. IF I COULD JUST GIVE HIM A *CHILD*, HE SAYS...

MY LADY...

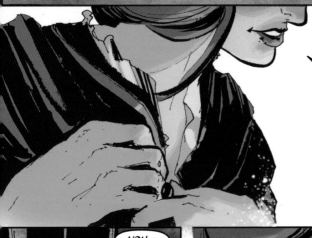

....I CAN GIVE YOU A CHILD.

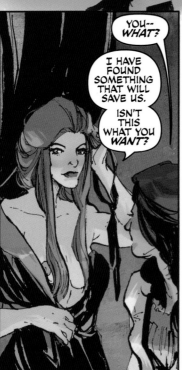

YOU-- *WHAT?*

I HAVE FOUND SOMETHING THAT WILL SAVE US. ISN'T THIS WHAT YOU *WANT?*

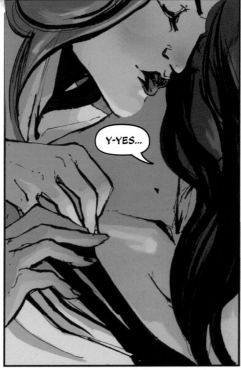

Y-YES...

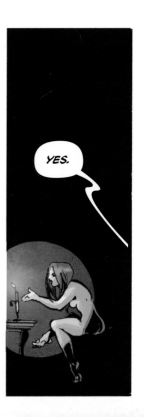

YES.

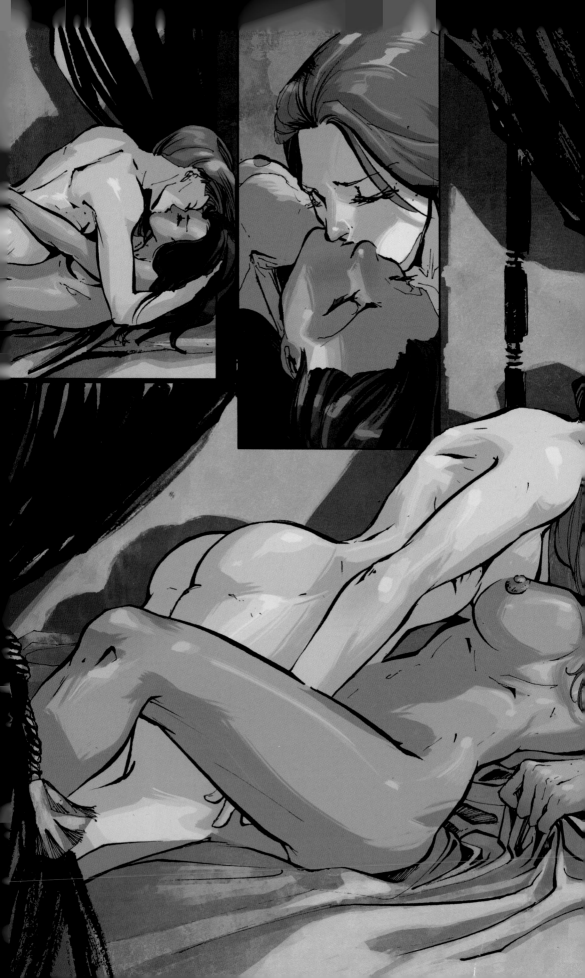

AH...
MFF!

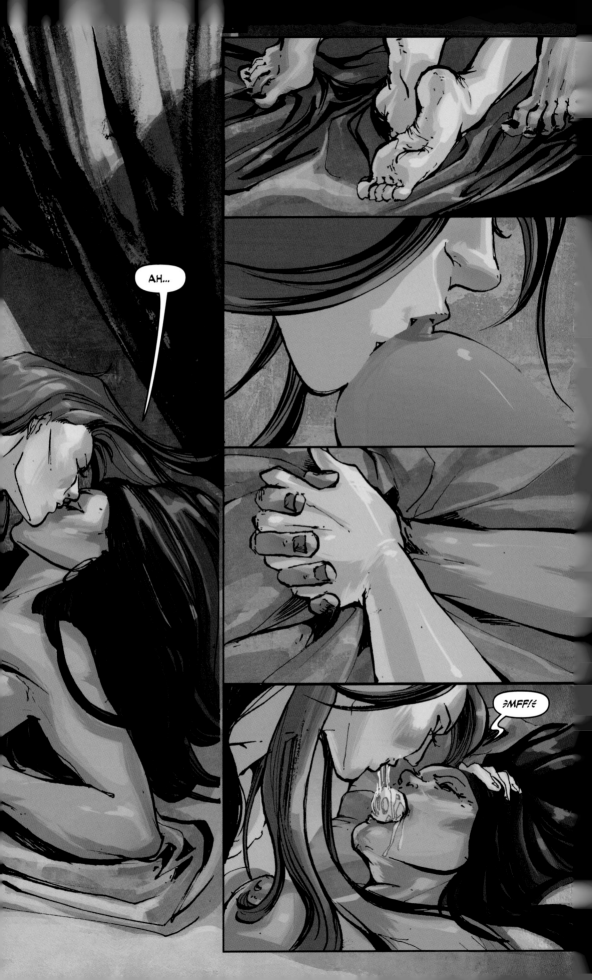

Ah!

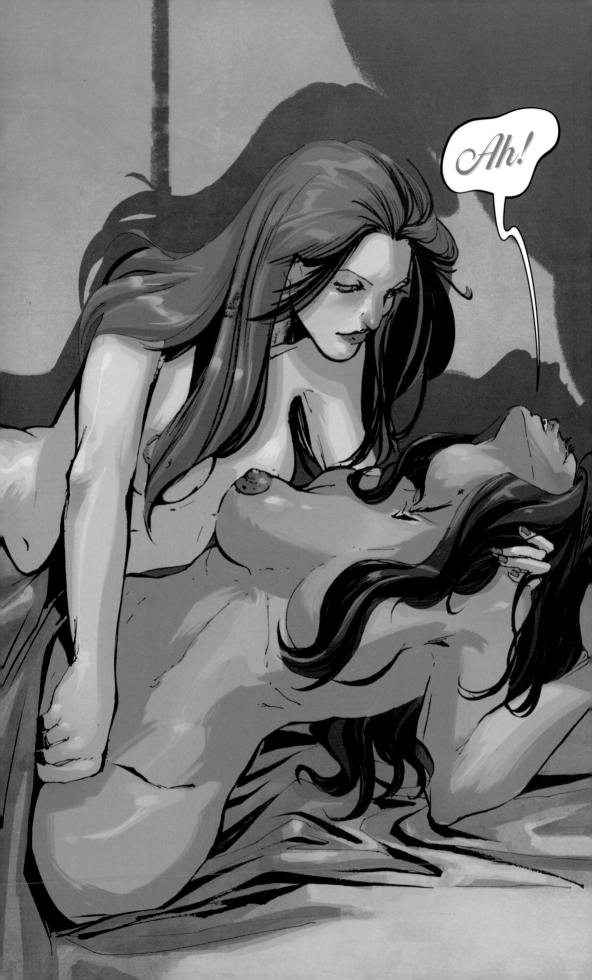

I FEEL... DIFFERENT.
ALL IS WELL, MY LADY. ALL IS WELL. SOON WE'LL BE TOGETHER...
...ONE HAPPY FAMILY.

LADY BERTRAM LOOKS RADIANT TONIGHT.
SPLENDID, SIMPLY SPLENDID.
OH, LADY BERTRAM! YOU COULD BRIGHTEN EVEN A LONDON FOG!

MAY WE EXPECT A *BLESSED EVENT* SOON?
NO NERVOUS FITS OF LATE?
NONE AT ALL, DR. TAYLOR. AND THANK YOU AGAIN FOR THE NOVEL! DID YOU ENJOY THE ONE I LENT YOU?
GHASTLY WORK-- SO NATURALLY I *ADORED* IT.
OH, I DO BEG YOUR PARDON, MY LADY, I SEE YOUR LORD HUSBAND--
I WISH IT WERE *YOU* DANCING WITH ME, MARIAH.
SOON, MY LADY. SOON. HOW IS YOUR DRESS?
TIGHT.
YOUR WIFE IS A ROSE, HARRY. SHE'S ALWAYS BEEN SO *KIND*, EVEN AFTER--
WILLIAM, *DON'T START.* YOU'RE A DOCTOR, NOT A--
WHY DO YOU REPEL HER THIS WAY?
SHE'S THE ONLY BUTTERFLY IN THIS NEST OF CATERPILLARS.
YES.
YES, SHE *IS.*

THAT'S ENOUGH FOR TONIGHT, MARIAH. I MEAN TO BE ALONE WITH MY *WIFE.*
IT'S BEEN *MONTHS,* HARRY. GROWING TIRED OF MOLESTING THE SERVANTS?
YOU'VE FOUND SOME BACKBONE SOMEWHERE, I'LL GIVE YOU *THAT.*
THAT MAID IS A SEDUCTRESS AND A LIAR.
AND ONLY A MAID, AND *ONLY IN NAME,* AFTER ALL.
YOU'RE THE THING I WANT.
"WANT"?
I WILL SHOW YOU THE MEANING OF *WANT.*

YES!
OH, GOD-- YOU'VE NEVER--YOU'VE NEVER--
URG
Agh!
HA HA HA HA...
GOOD NIGHT.

HURRRG
A TUMOR... NO, AN ULCER...
DAMN, WILLIAM! WHERE IS THE SOD WHEN YOU NEED HIM?!
YOU DID THIS! YOU'RE POISONING ME--
YOU WANT YOUR FORTUNE BACK, YOUR DOWRY, BUT YOU'LL NEVER GET IT, YOU BARREN WRETCH--
BLAM

WHERE DID IT COME FROM?
I KNEW A WOMAN... A LADY'S MAID TO AN OFFICER'S WIFE IN BURMA.
HE NEVER LET HER BE, KEPT HER WITH CHILD EVEN WHEN SHE SAID TOO MUCH, TOO MANY, TOO...
YOU KNOW, HARRY THUNDERED AND ROARED WHEN HE STUBBED A TOE, BUT I HAD TO HUSH EACH SOB AND SCREAM IN CHILDBED.
HE COULD CURSE AND RAIL WHEN HIS HORSE CAME THIRD, BUT WHEN I BURIED EVERY STILLBORN CHILD, I HAD TO SHOW DECORUM.
I WAS A WHORE IF I MET WILLIAM'S EYES, YET HENRY USED ALL THOSE POOR GIRLS IN THE SLUMS...
...AS IF HE WERE NOT MAKING THEM THE THINGS THEY BECAME.
NO LONGER, MY LOVE.
WE WILL BE THE REVENGE THEY COULD NOT TAKE.
WE WILL BE THE REVENGE WE ALL COULD NOT TAKE.
AAAAAAHHHH!

NO--
NO--!
AHHHH!
AAAAAAHH!

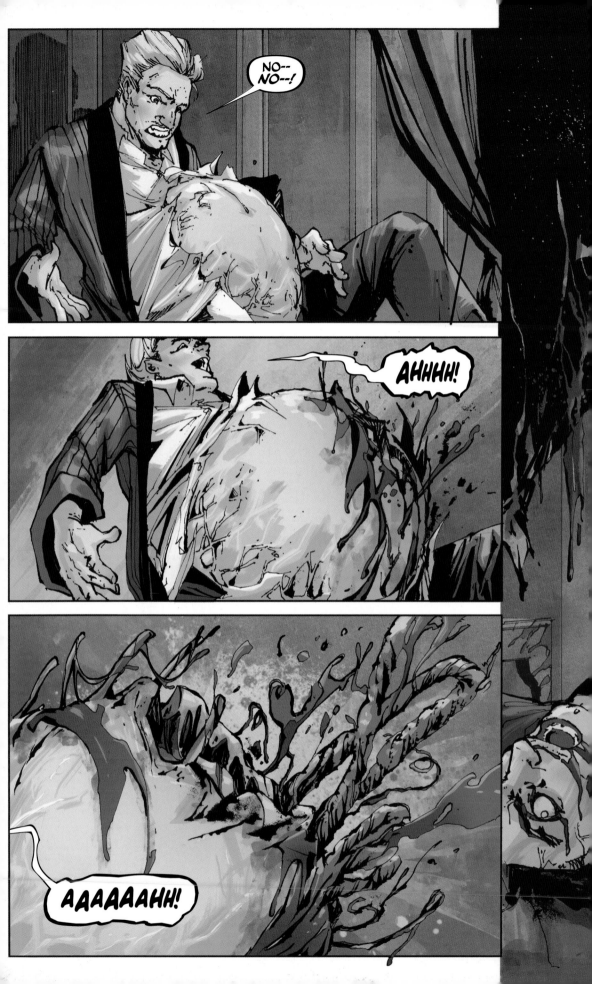

HKKT--

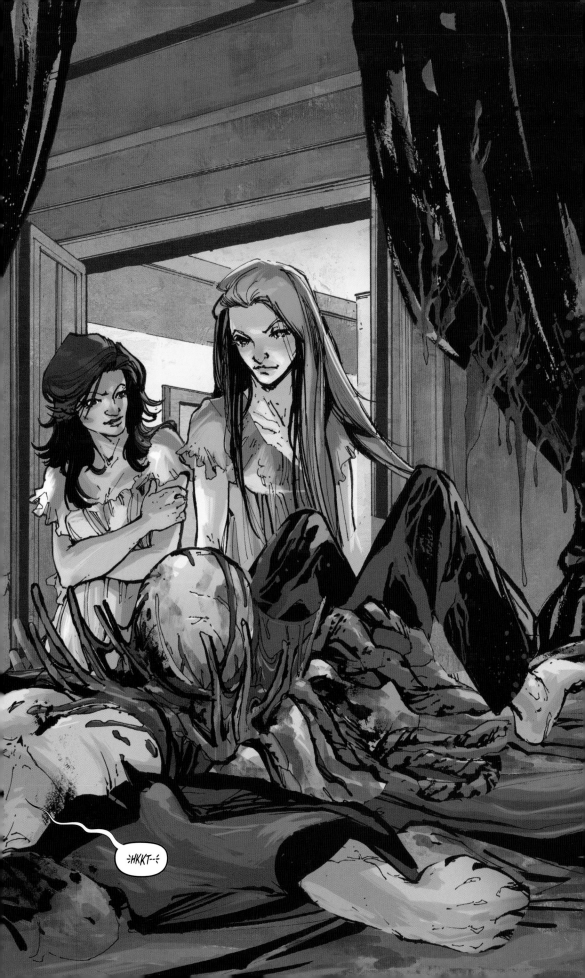

OH, MY LADY!
HE HAS YOUR HAIR!
AND YOUR EYES, MY SWEET.

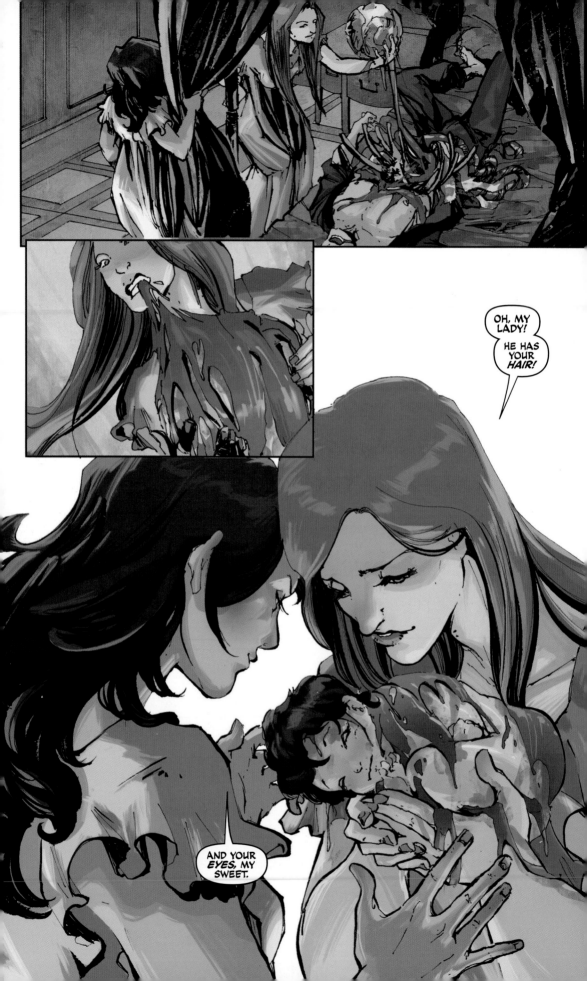

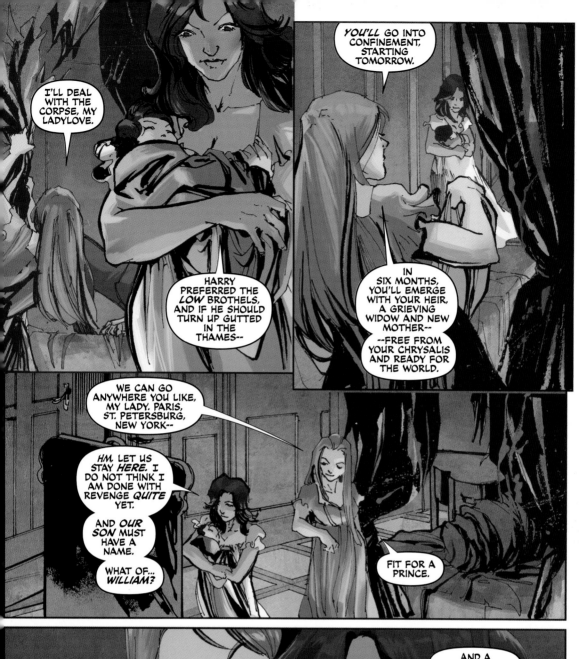

I'LL DEAL WITH THE CORPSE, MY LADYLOVE.

YOU'LL GO INTO CONFINEMENT, STARTING TOMORROW.

HARRY PREFERRED THE *LOW* BROTHELS, AND IF HE SHOULD TURN UP GUTTED IN THE THAMES--

IN SIX MONTHS, YOU'LL EMERGE WITH YOUR HEIR, A GRIEVING WIDOW AND NEW MOTHER--

--FREE FROM YOUR CHRYSALIS AND READY FOR THE WORLD.

WE CAN GO ANYWHERE YOU LIKE, MY LADY. PARIS, ST. PETERSBURG, NEW YORK--

HM. LET US STAY *HERE.* I DO NOT THINK I AM DONE WITH REVENGE *QUITE* YET.

AND *OUR SON* MUST HAVE A NAME.

WHAT OF... *WILLIAM?*

FIT FOR A PRINCE.

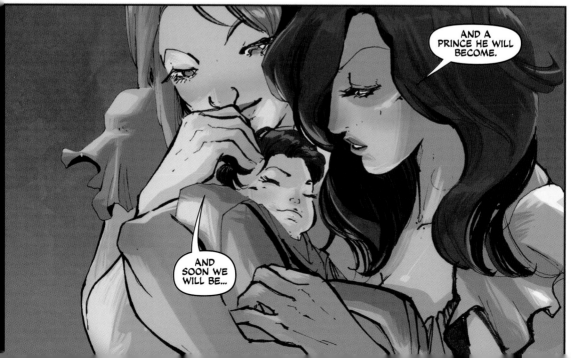

AND A PRINCE HE WILL BECOME.

AND SOON WE WILL BE...

...ONE HAPPY FAMILY.
NEXT:
InSEXts
CHAPTER II
Creeping things are changing, and in darkness descend -- let all of London tremble as our lovers take revenge

2

"GARDEN PARTY"

"THIS IS TORTURE, MARIAH...EVEN A NIGHT AWAY FROM OUR SON IS TORTURE."
"HE IS HAPPY WITH HIS NURSE, MY LADY.
"PERMIT YOURSELF BUT AN EVENING WITHOUT THESE FRETFUL NERVES, THESE HEAVY CARES YOU BEAR..."
"AHHH...IT IS SO HARD, BUT--AHHH...
"...MARIAH..."
"IT'S ALL RIGHT, MY DARLING..."

...LET GO.
...LET *EVERYTHING* GO.
MARIAH--!

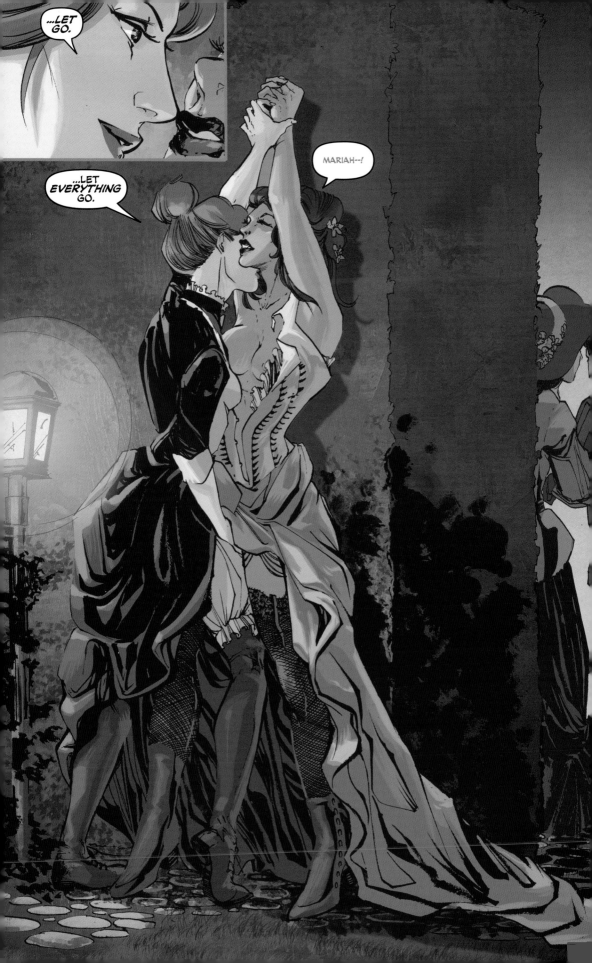

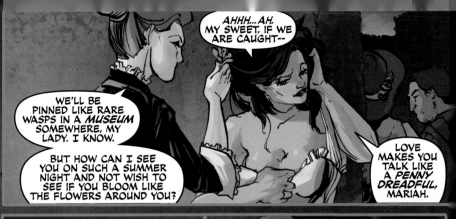

AHHH... AH. MY SWEET, IF WE ARE CAUGHT--

WE'LL BE PINNED LIKE RARE WASPS IN A *MUSEUM* SOMEWHERE, MY LADY. I KNOW.

BUT HOW CAN I SEE YOU ON SUCH A SUMMER NIGHT AND NOT WISH TO SEE IF YOU BLOOM LIKE THE FLOWERS AROUND YOU?

LOVE MAKES YOU TALK LIKE A *PENNY DREADFUL*, MARIAH.

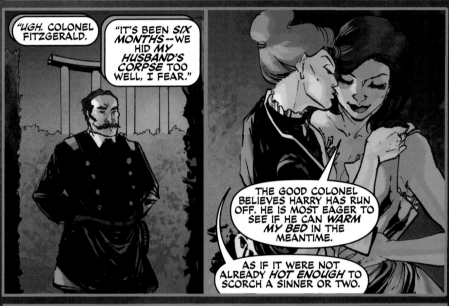

"UGH. COLONEL FITZGERALD.

"IT'S BEEN *SIX MONTHS* -- WE HID *MY HUSBAND'S CORPSE* TOO WELL, I FEAR."

THE GOOD COLONEL BELIEVES HARRY HAS RUN OFF. HE IS MOST EAGER TO SEE IF HE CAN *WARM MY BED* IN THE MEANTIME.

AS IF IT WERE NOT ALREADY *HOT ENOUGH* TO SCORCH A SINNER OR TWO.

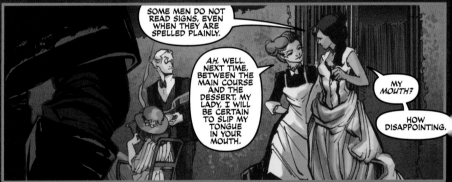

SOME MEN DO NOT READ SIGNS, EVEN WHEN THEY ARE SPELLED PLAINLY.

AH. WELL. NEXT TIME, BETWEEN THE MAIN COURSE AND THE DESSERT, MY LADY, I WILL BE CERTAIN TO SLIP MY TONGUE IN YOUR MOUTH.

MY MOUTH?

HOW DISAPPOINTING.

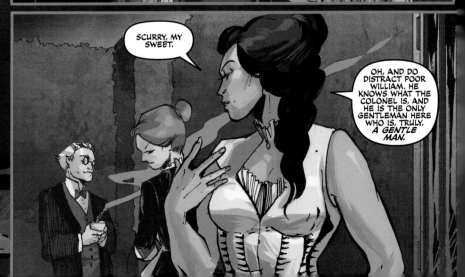

SCURRY, MY SWEET.

OH, AND DO DISTRACT POOR WILLIAM. HE KNOWS WHAT THE COLONEL IS, AND HE IS THE ONLY GENTLEMAN HERE WHO IS, TRULY, *A GENTLE MAN*.

I AM RELIEVED YOU FINALLY CAME TO YOUR SENSES, LADY BERTRAM. TEN TIMES I MUST HAVE ASKED YOU TO WALK WITH ME.
I BEGAN TO THINK YOU RUDE.
I HAVE OFTEN WONDERED HOW MANY OF US-- PARTICULARLY THE LADIES--ARE TRAPPED IN THINGS WE DO NOT WISH FOR OUT OF THE FEAR OF BEING BRANDED "RUDE."
AHHH, THE BUTTERFLIES LIKE YOU.
I LIKE YOU, TOO.
YET I'M SURE YOUR WIFE LIKES YOU MOST OF ALL.
THE RUMORS GO THAT YOUR HUSBAND HAS ABANDONED YOU. NO WAY TO TREAT A BRAHMIN WOMAN.
I HAVE SEEN EVEN THE INDIES. I ADMIRE THE WAYS OF YOUR PEOPLE.
I WAS BORN IN LONDON, COLONEL FITZGERALD.
THE WOMEN OF YOUR RANK ARE LIKE NOTHING ELSE EVER SEEN ON THIS EARTH.
AND NONE OF THEM ARE HALF SO INTOXICATING AS YOU. AN EXOTIC CREATURE--
"EXOTIC."
MY DEAR COLONEL...

...LET ME SHOW YOU HOW EXOTIC I CAN BE.
CHITTER
CHITTER
CHITTER

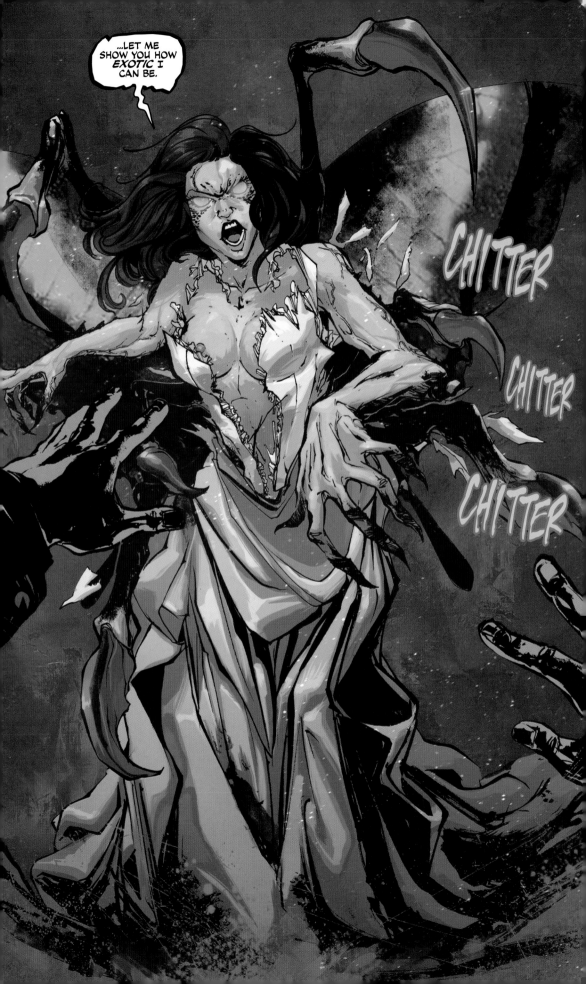

MARIAH! IT IS SUCH A PLEASURE TO SEE BOTH YOU AND LADY BERTRAM OUT IN SOCIETY AGAIN, AFTER THE MIRACULOUS EVENT.
YOU ARE MUCH TOO GOOD TO US, DR. TAYLOR. LADY'S SON IS GROWING LIKE A ROSE.
AND VULGAR AS IT IS TO SPEAK OF WEALTH, WITH YOUR MANAGEMENT OF OUR AFFAIRS DURING LORD BERTRAM'S--AH--JOURNEYS--
--MY LADY HAS YOU TO THANK FOR THE CHANGE IN OUR FORTUNES.
I--I KNOW HARRY HAS BEEN RATHER AN ABSENT FATHER THESE PAST FEW MONTHS. I'M SURE HE HAS HIS REASONS.
BUT IF THERE IS EVER ANY WAY I MIGHT BE OF ASSISTANCE--THAT IS TO SAY, IF LADY BERTRAM EVER HAD NEED OF--I MEAN--
YOU HAVE DONE US SUCH A KINDNESS ALREADY, SIR.
LADY CONSIDERS YOU HER MOST TRUSTED FRIEND.
LADIES AND GENTLEMEN! FORGIVE THE INTERRUPTION, PLEASE!
DR. TAYLOR?! IS THERE A DR. TAYLOR HERE?!
I AM HE--LAD, WHAT IS IT? WHAT IS THE CAUSE FOR THIS ALARM?
LADY.

MY LADY!
LADY--
MARIAH!
MARIAH, IT WAS AN ACCIDENT-- I COULDN'T CONTROL IT THIS TIME!
I MEANT ONLY TO FRIGHTEN HIM, BUT MY BODY--IT CHANGED, IT ALL CHANGED--
SHHH, SHHH, MY LADY, LET ME--
BE STILL. BE SOOTHED. THINK OF NOTHING. REMEMBER NOTHING.
BREATHE, INHALE THE SCENT... LIKE FLOWERS, LIKE POLLEN...
SHHHHH...

LADY! LADY BERTRAM! A MESSENGER HAS COME--
≈KOFF KOFF≈ WHAT THE DEVIL--
WILLIAM! D-DR. TAYLOR, I MEAN. IT IS NOT HOW IT APPEARS.
THE COLONEL... HAD A FIT. MY DRESS TORE AGAINST THE TRELLIS. MARIAH IS SEEING TO HIM.
PLEASE, I--
THANK YOU.
DR. TAYLOR, WHAT MESSENGER CAME?
I...LADY, DO FORGIVE ME...
...THERE HAS BEEN NEWS OF YOUR HUSBAND...
...HARRY HAS BEEN FOUND...

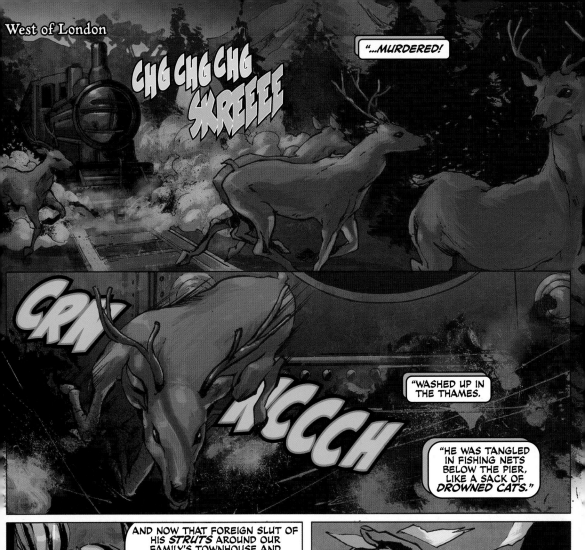

CHG CHG CHG
SKREEEE

"...MURDERED!

CRN

K'CCH

"WASHED UP IN
THE THAMES.

"HE WAS TANGLED
IN FISHING NETS
BELOW THE PIER,
LIKE A SACK OF
DROWNED CATS."

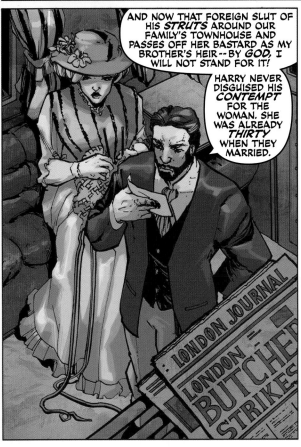

AND NOW THAT FOREIGN SLUT OF
HIS STRUTS AROUND OUR
FAMILY'S TOWNHOUSE AND
PASSES OFF HER BASTARD AS MY
BROTHER'S HEIR -- BY GOD, I
WILL NOT STAND FOR IT!

HARRY NEVER
DISGUISED HIS
CONTEMPT
FOR THE
WOMAN. SHE
WAS ALREADY
THIRTY
WHEN THEY
MARRIED.

LONDON JOURNAL

LONDON =
BUTCHER
STRIKES

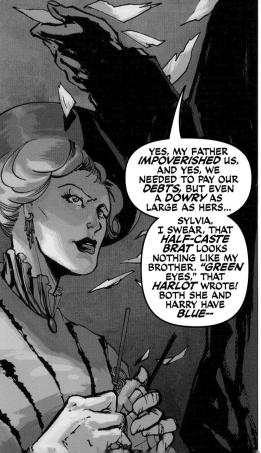

YES, MY FATHER
IMPOVERISHED US,
AND YES, WE
NEEDED TO PAY OUR
DEBTS, BUT EVEN
A DOWRY AS
LARGE AS HERS...

SYLVIA,
I SWEAR, THAT
HALF-CASTE
BRAT LOOKS
NOTHING LIKE MY
BROTHER. "GREEN
EYES," THAT
HARLOT WROTE!
BOTH SHE AND
HARRY HAVE
BLUE--

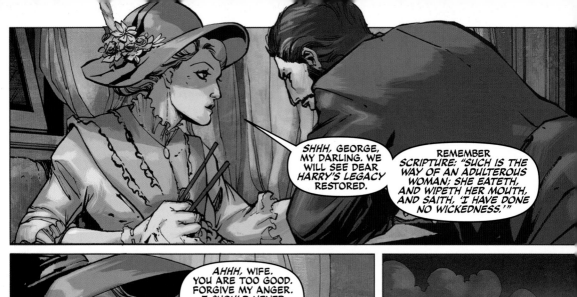

SHHH, GEORGE, MY DARLING. WE WILL SEE DEAR HARRY'S LEGACY RESTORED.

REMEMBER SCRIPTURE: "SUCH IS THE WAY OF AN ADULTEROUS WOMAN; SHE EATETH, AND WIPETH HER MOUTH, AND SAITH, 'I HAVE DONE NO WICKEDNESS.'"

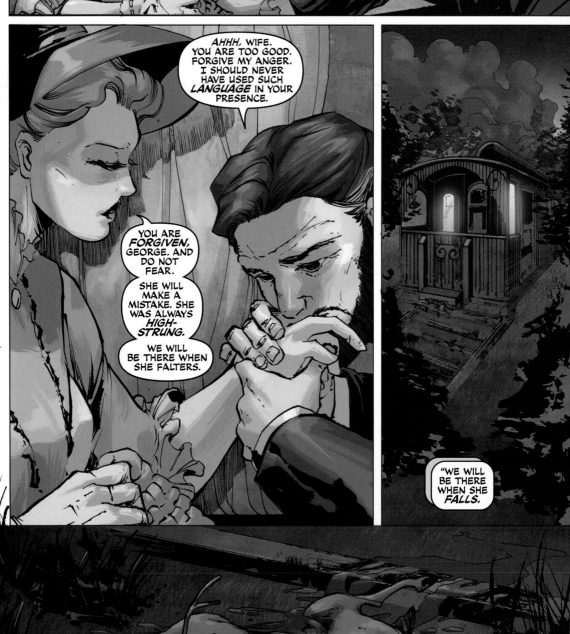

AHHH, WIFE. YOU ARE TOO GOOD. FORGIVE MY ANGER. I SHOULD NEVER HAVE USED SUCH *LANGUAGE* IN YOUR PRESENCE.

YOU ARE *FORGIVEN*, GEORGE. AND DO NOT FEAR.

SHE WILL MAKE A MISTAKE. SHE WAS ALWAYS *HIGH-STRUNG*.

WE WILL BE THERE WHEN SHE FALTERS.

"WE WILL BE THERE WHEN SHE *FALLS*."

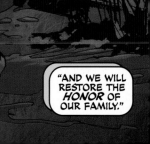

"AND WE WILL RESTORE THE *HONOR* OF OUR FAMILY."

The Bertram Townhouse
♫ TOO-RA-LOO-RA-LOO-RAL, TOO-RA-LOO-RA-LI... ♫
♫ TOO-RA-LOO-RA-LOO-RAL, HUSH, NOW DON'T YOU CRY... ♫
LOOK AT HIM, MARIAH...
EVERY DAY, HE IS MORE BEAUTIFUL, MORE OURS.
EVERY DAY, I LEARN ANEW WHAT IT MEANS FOR A THING TO BE PERFECT.
AYE, MY LADY. AND YOU'LL SEE HIS ROYAL PERFECTION AGAIN AFTER YOUR BATH.
TOO MUCH STRAIN MIGHT BRING ON ANOTHER, AH... FAINTING SPELL. I WOULD HAVE YOU CALM.
UGH, ALL THIS BLACK CRAPE! ALL THE MIRRORS COVERED, ALL THE WINDOWS CLOSED--
THE NICETIES MUST BE OBSERVED FOR THE TIME OF MOURNING, MY SWEET. OUR HOUSEHOLD, AT LEAST, IS SAFE.
THE OTHER SERVANTS ARE LOYAL TO US, AND KNEW WHAT HARRY WAS. NO ONE GRIEVES HIS PASSING HERE.

DO NOT SAY "THE OTHER SERVANTS," MY SWEET! YOU ARE NOT MY SERVANT--
I AM IF IT MEANS I'LL BE GETTING YOU OUT OF THAT ROBE AND INTO THIS TUB.
OH, NOW, ISN'T THAT THE PRETTIEST SIGHT IN CHRISTENDOM?
YOU NEEDN'T DO THAT EITHER, MY LOVE.
I LIKE DOING IT.
I LIKE TAKING CARE OF YOU.
AND WE ARE TRAPPED IN THIS HOUSE FOR THE NEXT SEVERAL MONTHS WHILE YOU MAKE EVERY APPEARANCE OF BEING IN DEEPEST MOURNING.
THE DEVIL I AM! I AM RESTLESS AND WILL ROAM WHERE I PLEASE, PLACES I HAVE NEVER BEEN PERMITTED BEFORE!
I AM QUITE CURIOUS TO SEE IF THESE WINGS LIVE UP TO ALL THEY PROMISE.
WE SHALL NOT BE CONFINED TO THIS PLACE, MY DOVE.
"OUR CHRYSALIS IS BROKEN"-- ISN'T THAT WHAT YOU SAID, THE NIGHT OUR BEAUTIFUL WILL WAS BORN?

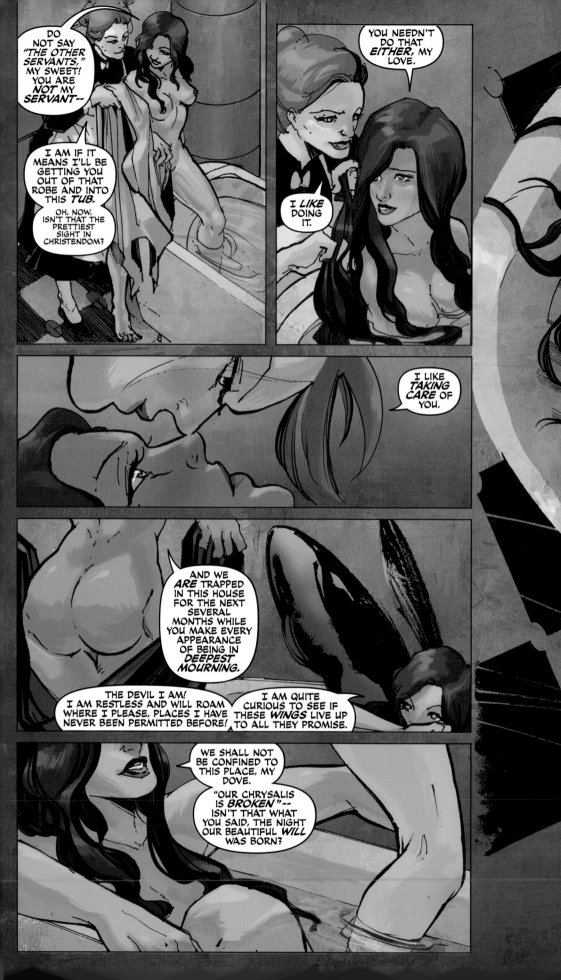

WE ARE FREE CREATURES, TO VENTURE WHERESOEVER WE PLEASE.
NO *WALLS* CAN IMPRISON US.
NO *TRADITIONS* CAN KEEP US CAGED...

"...NOTHING CAN CONFINE US ANY LONGER."
...FROM ROT THE BEAUTIES OF THE WORLD CAN ONLY EVER SPRING... FROM MISERY AND SORROW COMES THE MUSIC THAT WE SING...
THE SWEETEST SUMMER ROSES ARISE FROM SQUELCHING MUD
HERE, QUICK--
AND ALL GOD'S LITTLE CHILDREN ARE BORN TO US IN BLOOD
!
AND WE WHO LIVE TO SUFFER AS SEASONS BLOOM AND DIE
OH, YES--
KNOW THE HOPE OF EVERY CREEPING THING...
TO BE A BUTTERFLY...
AH. NO HARM.

HRRRRRHG
!!
GET DOWN! OH, GET DOWN!

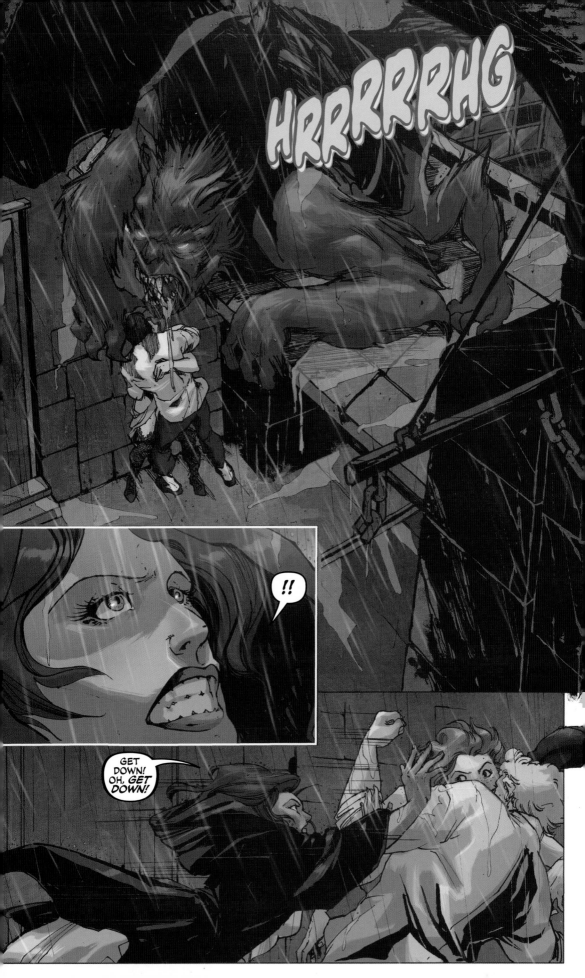

HRRRRRG
CHITTER CHITTER CHITTER
GRRRR...
WHAT WAS THAT?
OI! HATTIE! ARE YOU HURT?!
WAS IT THE LONDON BUTCHER?! DID YOU SEE 'IM?!

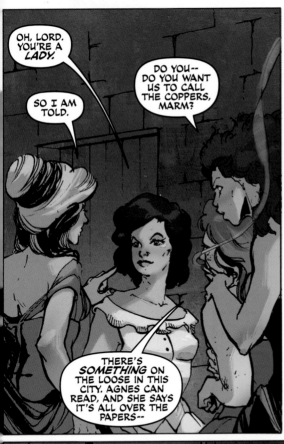

OH, LORD. YOU'RE A *LADY*.

SO I AM TOLD.

DO YOU-- DO YOU WANT US TO CALL THE COPPERS, MARM?

THERE'S *SOMETHING* ON THE LOOSE IN THIS CITY. AGNES CAN READ, AND SHE SAYS IT'S ALL OVER THE PAPERS--

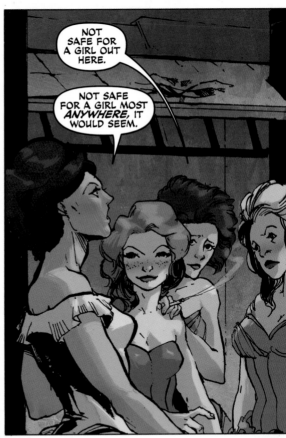

NOT SAFE FOR A GIRL OUT HERE.

NOT SAFE FOR A GIRL MOST *ANYWHERE*, IT WOULD SEEM.

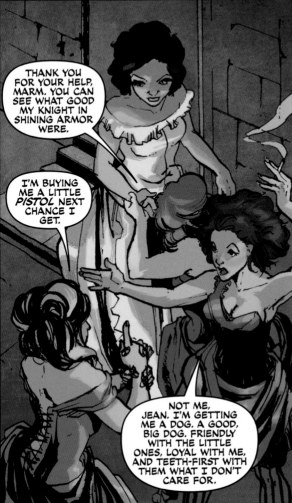

THANK YOU FOR YOUR HELP, MARM. YOU CAN SEE WHAT GOOD MY KNIGHT IN SHINING ARMOR WERE.

I'M BUYING ME A LITTLE *PISTOL* NEXT CHANCE I GET.

NOT ME, JEAN. I'M GETTING ME A DOG. A GOOD, BIG DOG. FRIENDLY WITH THE LITTLE ONES, LOYAL WITH ME, AND TEETH-FIRST WITH THEM WHAT I DON'T CARE FOR.

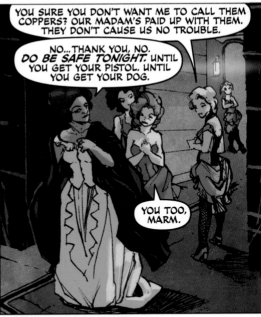

YOU SURE YOU DON'T WANT ME TO CALL THEM COPPERS? OUR MADAM'S PAID UP WITH THEM. THEY DON'T CAUSE US NO TROUBLE.

NO...THANK YOU, NO. *DO BE SAFE TONIGHT.* UNTIL YOU GET YOUR PISTOL. UNTIL YOU GET YOUR DOG.

YOU TOO, MARM.

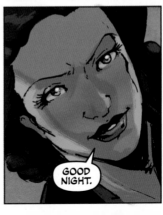

GOOD NIGHT.

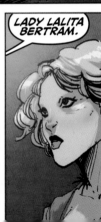

LADY LALITA BERTRAM.

...SYLVIA?!
YOU RECOGNIZE YOUR ERSTWHILE SISTER-IN-LAW, DO YOU? LALITA?
YOU KNOW NO ONE CALLS ME--NO, NEVER MIND. SYLVIA, WHAT ARE YOU DOING IN LONDON--?
THE FUNERAL, OF COURSE. FOR YOUR DEAD, MURDERED HUSBAND, IN CASE YOU HAD FORGOTTEN.
NOT IN MOURNING, I SEE.
COME SEEKING LOVERS, THEN?
TAKE CARE, SYLVIA. HARRY IS NOT ALIVE TO KEEP ME IN CHECK ANY LONGER.
AS I CAN SEE. NO LADY OF DECENT STANDING WOULD APPEAR IN A CESSPIT SUCH AS THIS, AT NIGHT, WITHOUT AN ESCORT, AND NOT EVEN IN MOURNING.
AND YET I SEE MORE THAN ONE LADY HERE TONIGHT.
YOUR TAINTED BLOOD WILL NOT SULLY OUR FAMILY.
I WILL SEE YOUR NAME DRAGGED THROUGH EVERY PAPER AND GUTTER. I WILL SEE YOU EXPOSED FOR THE MAD, UNNATURAL, RAVENOUS WHORE THAT YOU ARE.

THE ALIBIS OF YOUR RED-HAIRED WENCH CAN'T PROTECT YOU, LALITA. I HAVE FOUND HOLES IN YOUR STORY.
MY HUSBAND WILL SEE YOUR RECORDS--WHICH IS HIS RIGHT, AS FIRSTBORN, AS COUNT, AND NOT MERE VISCOUNT, LIKE DEAR DEPARTED HARRY.
WE WILL FIND THE TRUTH.
WHEN YOU WHELPED THAT PUKING, ILLEGITIMATE BRAT UNDER MY BROTHER-IN-LAW'S GOOD NAME...DID YOU CRAWL NAKED UNDER THE KITCHEN STOVE FIRST?
DID YOU GOBBLE DOWN THE AFTERBIRTH LIKE THE DOG-FACED BITCH YOU ARE?
I WILL SEE THOSE RIPE LIPS RIDDLED WITH SORES, WEEPING PUS...
...THAT LYING TONGUE WRAPPED AROUND THE PRICKS OF THE MEN FOR WHOM YOU BETRAYED OUR FAMILY'S HONOR.
I WILL SEE YOU END IN A BROTHEL LIKE THE ONE YOU HAVE SOUGHT TONIGHT.
I WILL SEE YOU SPREADING YOUR REEKING BLACK GASH TO SAILORS AND SOLDIERS AND DOGS.
I WILL SEE YOU SO HUNGRY, SO ABJECT, YOU WILL HAPPILY GO GAGGING, CHOKING, RETCHING ON THE SEED OF THE VERMIN OF THE EARTH.
I WILL SEE YOU EAT YOUR OWN FILTH TO SURVIVE.

AND WHEN YOU CAN BEAR NO MORE OF YOUR OWN PUTRESCENCE--
--I WILL SEE YOU, YOUR WENCH--
--AND YOUR BASTARD--
--STARVE.
GOOD NIGHT, LALITA.
IT'S GOOD TO BE HOME.
NEXT:
INSEXTS
CHAPTER III
Your chrysalis is broken
And vengeful works begin
But the sundered shell that freed you
Lets monsters slither in...

"THE NATURE OF WOMEN"
3

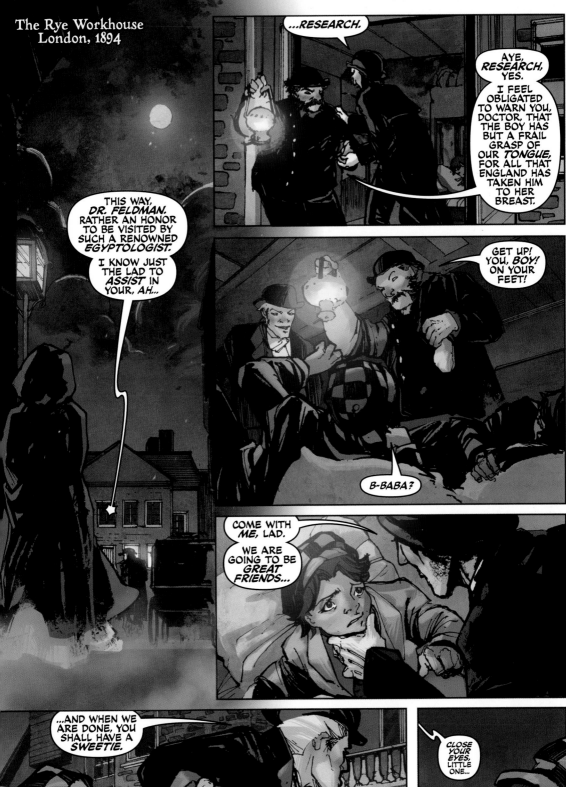

The Rye Workhouse
London, 1894

...RESEARCH.

AYE, *RESEARCH*, YES. I FEEL OBLIGATED TO WARN YOU, DOCTOR, THAT THE BOY HAS BUT A FRAIL GRASP OF OUR *TONGUE*, FOR ALL THAT ENGLAND HAS TAKEN HIM TO HER BREAST.

THIS WAY, *DR. FELDMAN.* RATHER AN HONOR TO BE VISITED BY SUCH A RENOWNED *EGYPTOLOGIST.* I KNOW JUST THE LAD TO *ASSIST* IN YOUR, AH...

GET UP! YOU, *BOY!* ON YOUR FEET!

B-BABA?

COME WITH *ME*, LAD. WE ARE GOING TO BE *GREAT* FRIENDS...

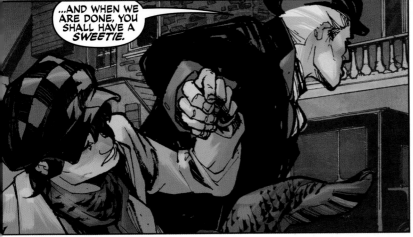

...AND WHEN WE ARE DONE, YOU SHALL HAVE A *SWEETIE.*

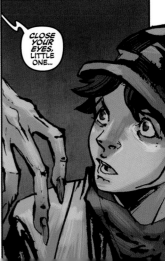

CLOSE YOUR EYES, LITTLE ONE...

...THERE IS NOTHING *SWEETER* THAN *THIS.*
WHRRRNHN
AIIIIEEEE--
SKRRKT SQUOLCH
OH, THERE'S A GOOD BOY, HAKIM.
KEEP YOUR EYES ON ME AND YOU *SHALL* HAVE A *SWEETIE.*
I PROMISE, THEY ARE MUCH BETTER...

"...WHEN YOUR *MOTHER* HAS MADE THEM."
The Bertram Household
London
HAKIM!
MAMA! BABA!
AT THE RATE YOU'RE GOING, MY JOY, YOU'RE GOING TO MAKE OUR *TAILOR* RICHER THAN *CROESUS.*
COULD YOU *CONTROL IT* THIS TIME?
THANK YOU, MARIAH. *THANK YOU.*
I DON'T KNOW HOW YOU FOUND OUR HAKIM, HOW YOU KNEW WHERE TO *LOOK,* YOU AND OUR LADY--
ALWAYS, RANYA, ADOM-- WE'RE JUST GLAD HE'S HOME AGAIN.
I DON'T KNOW HOW ON EARTH THE POLICE EVER PICKED HIM UP--
--WE ARE LUCKY THE POLICE AREN'T AFTER *YOU,* MY LADY, WITH *THE LONDON BUTCHER* RUNNING ABOUT--
--AND WITH *YOUR GHASTLY IN-LAWS* SLEEPING IN THE EAST WING, IT'S A WONDER HARRY'S RELATIVES HAVEN'T TURNED ME IN FOR A CATHOLIC SPY AND YOU FOR THE BRIDE OF THE *DEVIL.*
OH, MARIAH.
THE THINGS WE DO FOR *FAMILY.*
OH, YES...

"...WHAT THINGS INDEED."
YOU KNOW, MARIAH... I KEEP THINKING OF THAT DREADFUL WORKHOUSE WHERE HAKIM WAS TAKEN.
AND I DO WORRY OF THE EFFECT OF THESE FREQUENT TRANSFORMATIONS.
WE HAVE BEEN CHANGING SO RAPIDLY THESE PAST FEW MONTHS, AND NOT ALWAYS IN WAYS WE INTEND.
WELL, I CANNOT EXACTLY GO TO SWEET WILLIAM AND ASK FOR A PHYSICAL EXAMINATION, DARLING--
NO. THOUGH TAKING HIM INTO OUR CONFIDENCE IS NOT A TERRIBLE IDEA, EITHER.
I DO BELIEVE HIS INFLUENCE WAS ALL THAT PREVENTED OUR LIVES WITH HARRY FROM BEING ABSOLUTELY UNENDURABLE.
DR. TAYLOR WOULD DO ANYTHING FOR YOU--INCLUDING, I BELIEVE, KEEP OUR SECRETS.
THAT YOU CANNOT SAVE EVERY SOUL IN LONDON DOES NOT MEAN THE GOOD YOU MANAGE IS WORTHLESS, MY LADY.
"...I CAN SMELL THE CHAMBERMAID TRYSTING WITH THE GROOM IN THE STABLES...

AND WITH HIS KNOWLEDGE OF *ANATOMY,* MAYBE HE WOULD HAVE *INSIGHT* INTO WHAT WE ARE UNDERGOING.
I *WORRY* FOR HIM, MARIAH. AS MUCH AS HE EVER WORRIED FOR ME.
IF I WERE TO TRANSFORM AROUND HIM, AND *LOSE CONTROL...*
WELL, THE *SPONTANEOUS ARMS* REMAIN RATHER A CONCERN.
THEY ARE EVIDENCE AGAINST US, AND *DRY AS HUSKS,* SO DO MIND WHERE YOU SHED THEM, MY DOVE.
THAT *CLOUD OF SCENT* YOU RELEASED ON THE UNLUCKY COLONEL AT THE GARDEN PARTY, AFTER HIS, AH--*ENCOUNTER* WITH ME--
--WHAT *WAS* THAT, MARIAH?
MY BODY DOESN'T TRANSFORM IN THE SAME WAY AS YOURS.
MY SENSES ARE *SHARP,* THOUGH...
"...I CAN SMELL THE FRUIT AND HONEY THAT RANYA AND THE SCULLERY MAIDS HAVE BROUGHT IN FOR OUR BREAKFAST...
"...JUST AS I COULD SMELL THE SCENT OF YOUR *PANIC,* THAT NIGHT IN THE HEDGE MAZE...
"...JUST AS I COULD SENSE *HAKIM,* THROUGH THE FOG AND GLOOM OF LONDON..."
...I COULD FOLLOW YOUR TRAIL.
I KNEW *EXACTLY* WHERE YOU WERE.
WE ARE BECOME *NEW CREATURES,* MY LOVE.
GHASTLY PENNY DREADFULS SPEAK OF VAMPIRES AND WEREWOLVES, GHOULS AND GOBLINS--
--YET THERE ARE *NO MONSTERS* LIKE *US.*

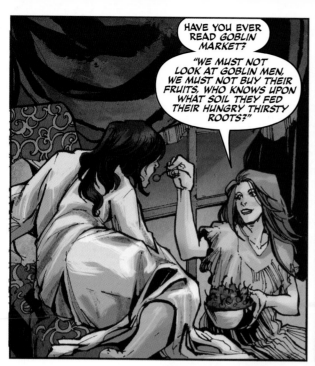

HAVE YOU EVER READ *GOBLIN MARKET?*

"WE MUST NOT LOOK AT GOBLIN MEN, WE MUST NOT BUY THEIR FRUITS, WHO KNOWS UPON WHAT SOIL THEY FED THEIR HUNGRY THIRSTY ROOTS?"

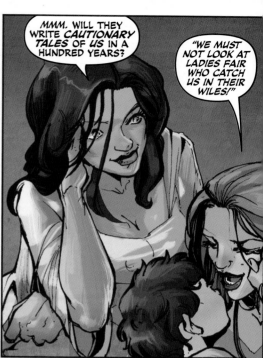

MMM. WILL THEY WRITE *CAUTIONARY TALES* OF *US* IN A HUNDRED YEARS?

"WE MUST NOT LOOK AT LADIES FAIR WHO CATCH US IN THEIR WILES!"

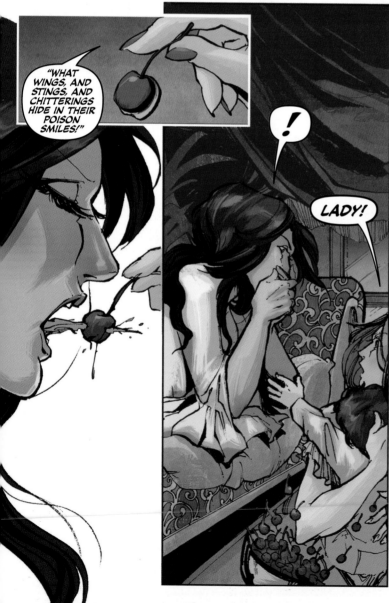

"WHAT WINGS, AND STINGS, AND CHITTERINGS HIDE IN THEIR POISON SMILES!"

!

LADY!

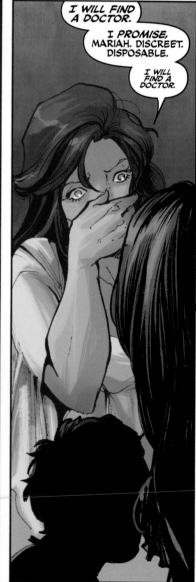

I WILL FIND A DOCTOR.

I PROMISE, MARIAH. DISCREET. DISPOSABLE.

I WILL FIND A DOCTOR.

White Chapel

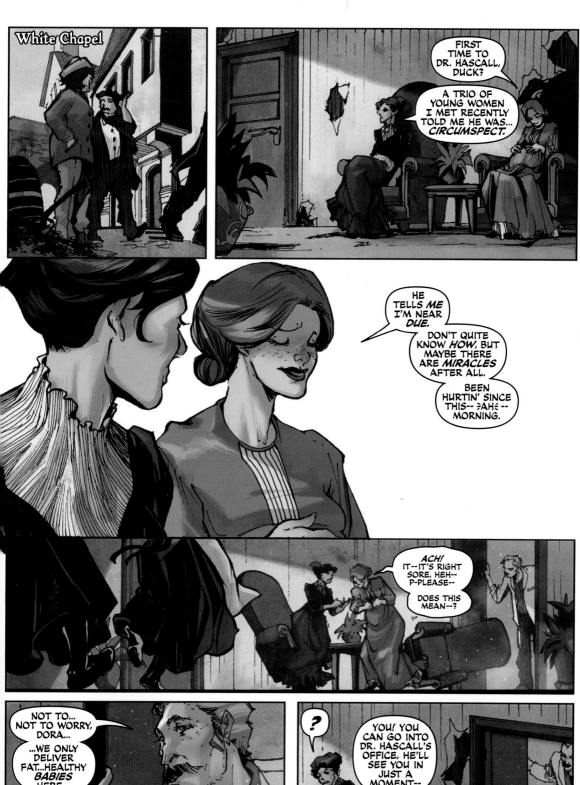

FIRST TIME TO DR. HASCALL, DUCK?

A TRIO OF YOUNG WOMEN I MET RECENTLY TOLD ME HE WAS... *CIRCUMSPECT.*

HE TELLS *ME* I'M NEAR *DUE.*

DON'T QUITE KNOW *HOW,* BUT MAYBE THERE ARE *MIRACLES* AFTER ALL.

BEEN HURTIN' SINCE THIS-- ?AH?-- MORNING.

ACH! IT--IT'S RIGHT SORE, HEH-- P-PLEASE--

DOES THIS MEAN--?

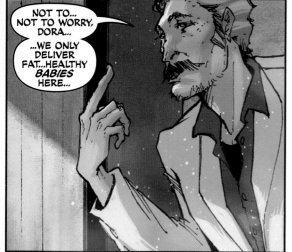

NOT TO... NOT TO WORRY, DORA...

...WE ONLY DELIVER FAT...HEALTHY *BABIES* HERE...

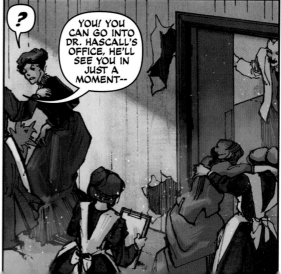

?

YOU! YOU CAN GO INTO DR. HASCALL'S OFFICE, HE'LL SEE YOU IN JUST A MOMENT--

DISCREET AND DISPOSABLE, THAT'S WHAT YOU ASKED FOR IN A DOCTOR, LADY.
DISCREET AND DISPOSABLE... NO MORE THAN HARRY CHOOSING THOSE POOR GIRLS IN THE SLUMS.
?
!!

OPIUM.
DORA! DORA!
THE DOCTOR HAS TAKEN OPIUM, HE DOESN'T--
!
NURSE!
N-NURSE!

The Bertram Household
LAD.
OH, AN UPSET TUMMY?
TOO MANY SWEETIES?
TOO MUCH OF A GOOD THING IS A SIN, YOU KNOW.
DO YOU WANT TO LIVE IN SIN? NO?
DID YOU KNOW THAT ANYONE CAN PERFORM A BAPTISM IN CRISIS, LITTLE LAMB?
IF THE PERSON'S MORTAL SOUL IS IN PERIL.
AS YOURS IS, IN A HOUSE WITH THOSE CREATURES.
COUNTESS BERTRAM.
WHY DON'T YOU COME WITH ME?
WE'LL GET YOU NICE AND CLEAN.

RUN ALONG TO YOUR PARENTS, HAKIM.
THE BERTRAM ESTATE IS NOT ENTAILED, COUNTESS.
YOU HAVE NO POWER HERE.
MM, I'M NOT QUITE SURE THAT IS TRUE.
TELL ME-- WERE YOU THE ONE WHO SAW TO IT THAT HAKIM WAS LED INTO THE STREET?
HA.
I WAS CURIOUS WHAT YOU WOULD DO.
WHY DO YOU HATE MY LADY, COUNTESS?
YOUR LADY DOES NOT HAVE THE GRACE TO BE GRATEFUL FOR THE GIFT OF HER WOMANHOOD.
IT WAS NOT ENOUGH TO RIDE IN A FINE CARRIAGE AND WEAR BEAUTIFUL THINGS, TO BE PROTECTED FROM POVERTY, FROM REALITY, FROM THE DANGER OF THE WORLD.
IT WAS NOT ENOUGH TO BE BORN A HALF-BREED AND YET ASCEND THROUGH THE PEERAGE OF LONDON.
IT IS THE NATURE OF WOMEN TO BE DISCONTENT-- TO HUNGER, TO LUST, TO SHAME, AND TO PRY.
YOUR LADY MIGHT'VE BEEN ADORED IF SHE WERE GRATEFUL FOR THE ATTENTIONS OF SO FINELY BRED A HUSBAND.
SO ADORED THAT HER HUSBAND WED HER FOR HER DOWRY, COUNTESS?

WOMEN HAVE THE CHANCES TO BE THE ANGELS OF THE HOUSE-- VIRGINS, WIVES, MOTHERS, GRACE INCARNATE--
--YET THEY ARE UNGRATEFUL.
THEY EMASCULATE THOSE THEY SHOULD HONOR AND PROTECT, THEN SHAME THEM, THEN CRY WHEN THEY ARE GIVEN WHAT THEY DESERVE.
IT IS NATURE.
SPITE IS THE NATURE OF WOMEN. TO BE DISSATISFIED. TO BE DISOBEDIENT.
EVE IN THE GARDEN, THE MOTHER OF SIN-- DELILAH, A LIAR AND SEDUCTRESS-- JEZEBEL, QUEEN OF ABOMINATIONS--
--PRYING PANDORA, UNLEASHING GRIEF ON THE WORLD.
YOU MIGHT TRY A FEW EXAMPLES THAT ACTUALLY HAPPENED, COUNTESS BERTRAM.
HISTORY IS FILLED WITH THE WEAKNESS OF WOMEN.
AND HISTORY, BY AND LARGE, IS WRITTEN BY MEN.
?
!
HOW DID YOU--?
...LYE.

CRSH
YOU ASP!
YOU VIPER--!
AHH!
LISTEN TO ME, COUNTESS.
IF YOU TRY TO TOUCH LADY'S SON--
--I WILL GUT YOU BLOODY.
TRY TO THREATEN LADY. TRY TO FRIGHTEN CHILDREN.
BUT KNOW-- NOTHING FRIGHTENS ME.
BANG
IS...IS THAT SO?
MY LADY!

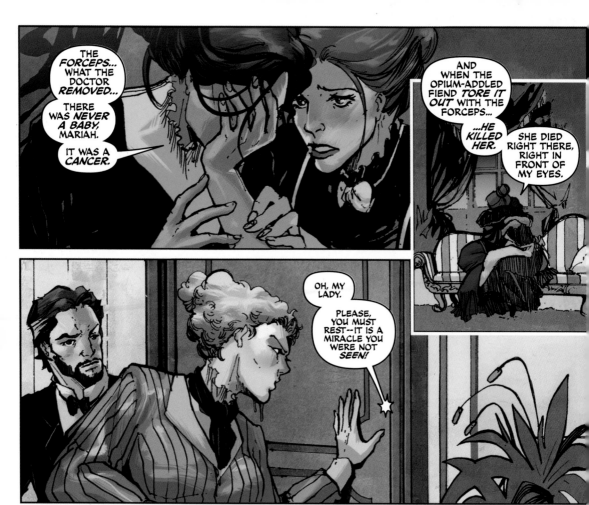

THE FORCEPS... WHAT THE DOCTOR REMOVED...

THERE WAS NEVER A BABY, MARIAH.

IT WAS A CANCER.

AND WHEN THE OPIUM-ADDLED FIEND TORE IT OUT WITH THE FORCEPS...

...HE KILLED HER.

SHE DIED RIGHT THERE, RIGHT IN FRONT OF MY EYES.

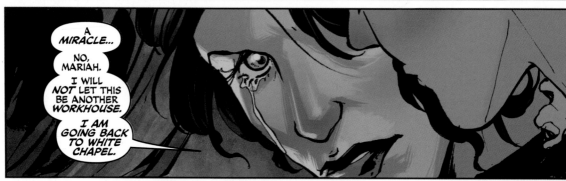

OH, MY LADY.

PLEASE, YOU MUST REST--IT IS A MIRACLE YOU WERE NOT SEEN!

A MIRACLE...

NO, MARIAH.

I WILL NOT LET THIS BE ANOTHER WORKHOUSE.

I AM GOING BACK TO WHITE CHAPEL.

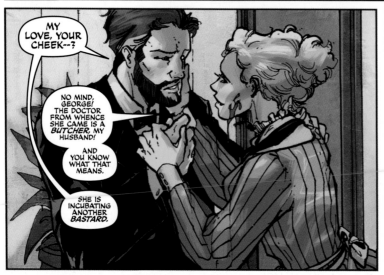

MY LOVE, YOUR CHEEK--?

NO MIND, GEORGE! THE DOCTOR FROM WHENCE SHE CAME IS A BUTCHER, MY HUSBAND!

AND YOU KNOW WHAT THAT MEANS.

SHE IS INCUBATING ANOTHER BASTARD.

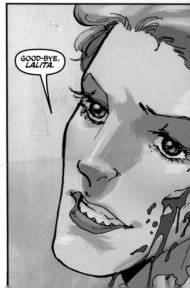

GOOD-BYE, LALITA.

White Chapel Night
THANK YOU FOR SEEING ME ON SUCH SHORT NOTICE, DR. HASCALL.
I HAVE BEEN EXPERIENCING THE MOST PECULIAR INSTINCTS.
THE... THE MONEY...
YESSSS, THE MONEY.
THAT'S WHAT YOU CARE ABOUT, NOT THE WOMEN.
WELL, I HAVE LOTS OF MONEY, DR. HASCALL.
TO KEEP US AWAY...
...FROM PRYING EYES.

YOURS IS...IS NOT A CASE OF PREGNANCY, MY DEAR...
...BUT OF HYSTERIA... BROUGHT ON BY A...WANDERING WOMB.
THE...WOMB IS...UNLIKE OTHER ORGANS... IT CHANGES... TRAVELS...
WHAT MUST I DO, DOCTOR?
AFFLICTED WOMEN MUST... TAKE A HUSBAND... PRODUCE CHILDREN...
...ANCHOR THE WOMB...
...IN ITS PROPER PLACE...
?!
MY ARM--MY ARM--?!

AHHH!
CRWNCH
SKRONCH
CRNNCH

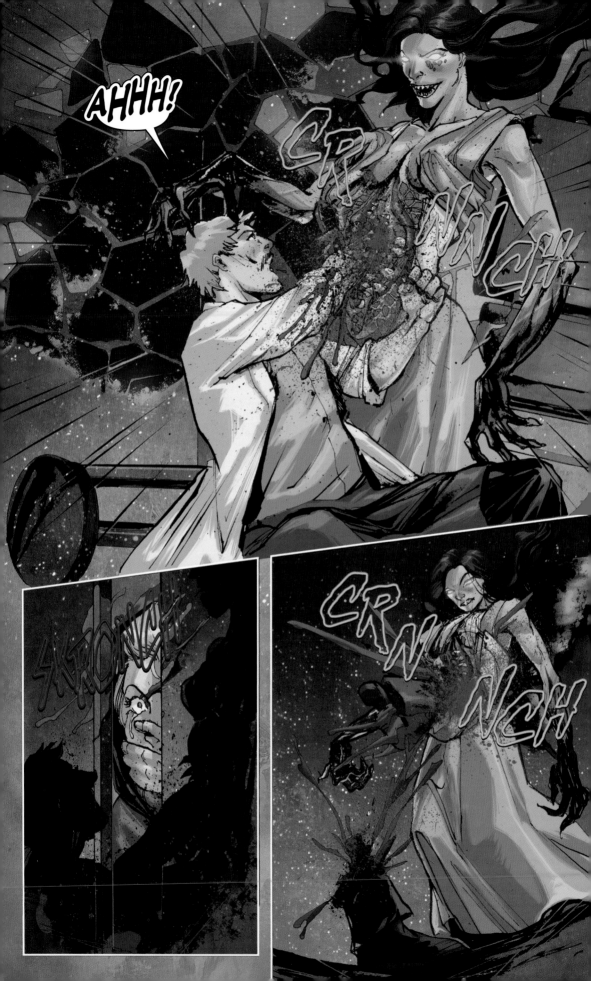

GASP
PANT PANT
OH, YOU SWEET LITTLE BITCH...
...GIVE ME WHAT I WANT...
GIVE
ME

WHAT DID YOU DO WITH THE *NURSES*, MY LADY?

≥SIGH≤
THEY WILL LIVE... BUT THERE WILL BE NO MORE OF THEIR KIND OF *MIRACLES* IN WHITE CHAPEL.

BANG BANG

BANG BANG BANG

WHAT UNDER HEAVEN--

DR. TAYLOR! DO YOU KNOW WHAT HOUR OF THE NIGHT--?!

PLEASE, ADOM, I MUST SPEAK WITH *LADY BERTRAM.*
LADY BERTRAM! *LADY--*

FORGIVE ME, MY LADY.
THEY... THEY HAVE FOUND *YOUR HUSBAND'S MURDERER!*

THE MAN *TURNED HIMSELF IN* TO SCOTLAND YARD TODAY, FOR *HARRY'S DEATH*, FOR A DOZEN OTHERS...
...THE WRETCH *CONFESSED* TO BEING...
...*THE LONDON BUTCHER!*

NEXT:
INSEXTS
CHAPTER IV

4

"HUNTERS"

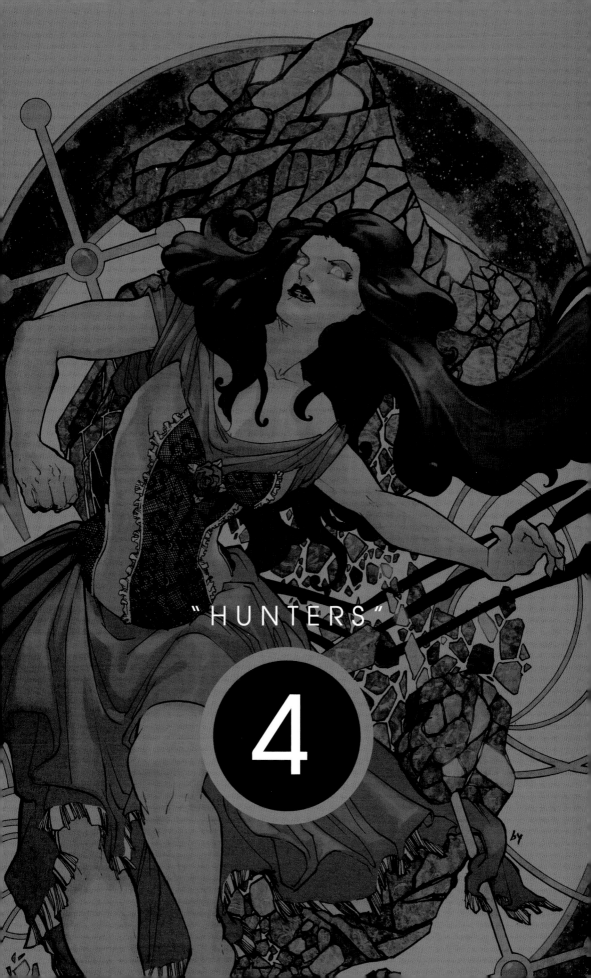

London, 1894.
The Bertram Townhouse.
PLEASE, MY LADY, THINK THIS THROUGH--
YOU SAY THE *LONDON BUTCHER* HAS BEEN CAUGHT-- HAS *CONFESSED* TO MY *HUSBAND'S MURDER.*
I WOULD LOOK IN THE FACE OF THE MAN WHO CLAIMS--WHO *ADMITS* SUCH A THING.
WATCH OVER MY SON, MARIAH.
OUR SON.
DON'T LET HIM OUT OF YOUR SIGHT.
"NOT WITH MY VICIOUS *ASP* OF A SISTER-IN-LAW SLITHERING AROUND OUR HOUSE.
"WE MUST FIND A WAY TO DEAL WITH DEAR *SYLVIA,* AND SOON."
I WISH YOU WOULD RECONSIDER, MY LADY.
I CAN'T, WILLIAM. I MUST KNOW WHO THIS MAN IS.
THE MAN WHO HAS FALSELY ADMITTED TO KILLING THE HUSBAND *YOU MURDERED?*
WILLIAM!
CLK

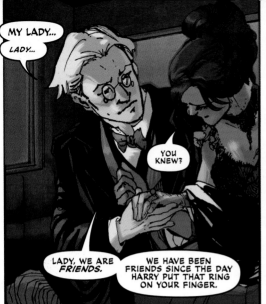

MY LADY...

LADY...

YOU KNEW?

LADY, WE ARE *FRIENDS.*

WE HAVE BEEN FRIENDS SINCE THE DAY HARRY PUT THAT RING ON YOUR FINGER.

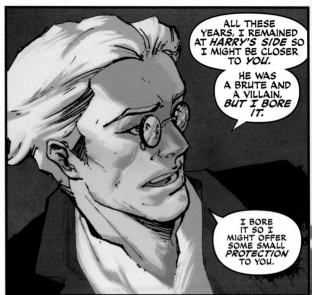

ALL THESE YEARS, I REMAINED AT *HARRY'S SIDE* SO I MIGHT BE CLOSER TO *YOU.*

HE WAS A BRUTE AND A VILLAIN, *BUT I BORE IT.*

I BORE IT SO I MIGHT OFFER SOME SMALL *PROTECTION* TO YOU.

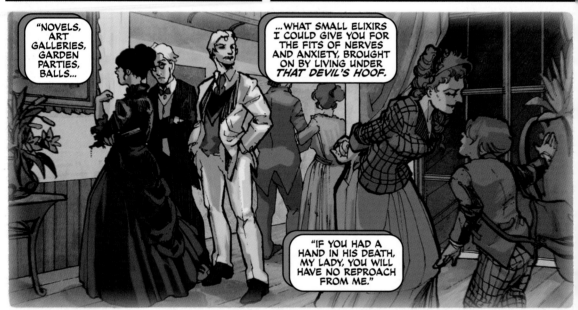

"NOVELS, ART GALLERIES, GARDEN PARTIES, BALLS...

...WHAT SMALL ELIXIRS I COULD GIVE YOU FOR THE FITS OF NERVES AND ANXIETY, BROUGHT ON BY LIVING UNDER *THAT DEVIL'S HOOF.*

"IF YOU HAD A HAND IN HIS DEATH, MY LADY, YOU WILL HAVE NO REPROACH FROM ME."

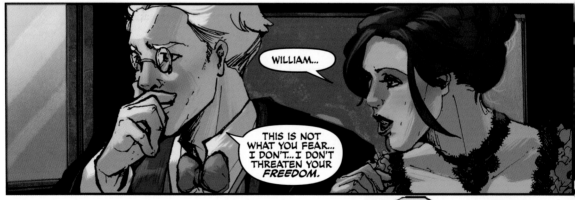

WILLIAM...

THIS IS NOT WHAT YOU FEAR... I DON'T... I DON'T THREATEN YOUR *FREEDOM.*

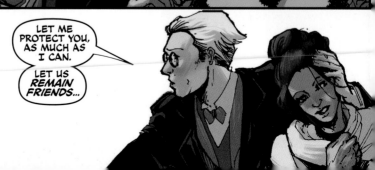

LET ME PROTECT YOU, AS MUCH AS I CAN.

LET US *REMAIN FRIENDS...*

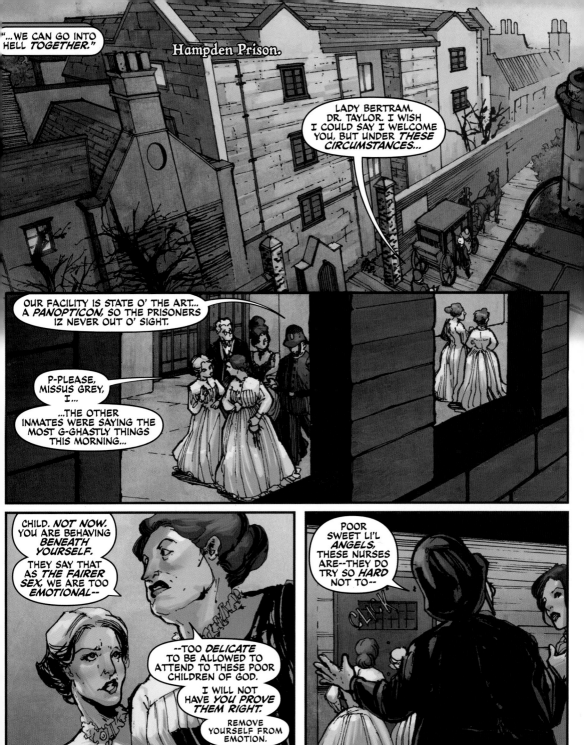

"...WE CAN GO INTO HELL *TOGETHER.*"

Hampden Prison.

LADY BERTRAM. DR. TAYLOR. I WISH I COULD SAY I WELCOME YOU, BUT UNDER *THESE* CIRCUMSTANCES...

OUR FACILITY IS STATE O' THE ART... A *PANOPTICON,* SO THE PRISONERS IZ NEVER OUT O' SIGHT.

P-PLEASE, MISSUS GREY, I...

...THE OTHER INMATES WERE SAYING THE MOST G-GHASTLY THINGS THIS MORNING...

CHILD. *NOT NOW.* YOU ARE BEHAVING *BENEATH YOURSELF.*

THEY SAY THAT AS *THE FAIRER SEX,* WE ARE TOO *EMOTIONAL*--

--TOO *DELICATE* TO BE ALLOWED TO ATTEND TO THESE POOR CHILDREN OF GOD.

I WILL NOT HAVE *YOU PROVE THEM RIGHT.*

REMOVE YOURSELF FROM EMOTION.

POOR SWEET LI'L *ANGELS,* THESE NURSES ARE--THEY DO TRY SO *HARD* NOT TO--

CLICK

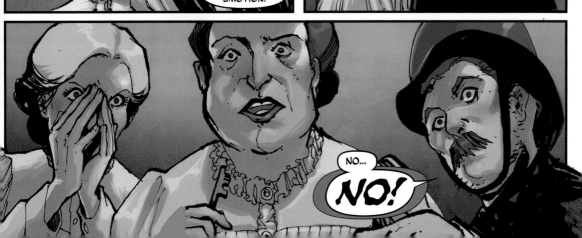

NO...

NO!

HELP! HEEELP!
HE BUTCHERED THEM! HE EN'T HUMAN!
WE SCREAMED AND NO ONE CAME--
WE SCREAMED AND NO ONE CAME!

HHHRK
LADY!
NO-- N-N-N--
!
IT'S-- IT'S A FIT! ONLY A FIT...
I AM HER DOCTOR! CALL THE CARRIAGE AT ONCE!
AT ONCE, DAMN YOU!
I WON'T LET ANYTHING HURT YOU.
NOT EVEN THIS.

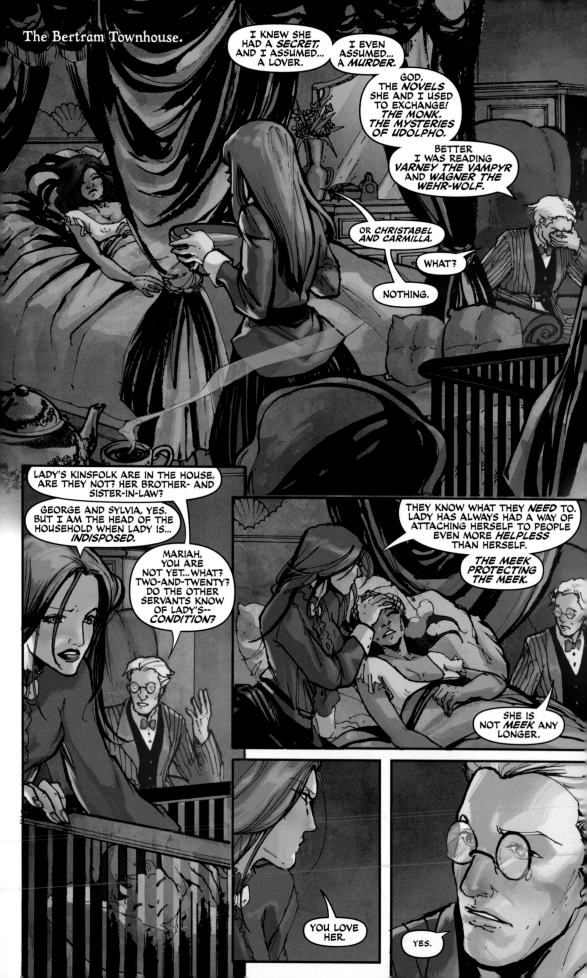

The Bertram Townhouse.

I KNEW SHE HAD A *SECRET*, AND I ASSUMED... A LOVER.

I EVEN ASSUMED... A *MURDER*.

GOD, THE *NOVELS* SHE AND I USED TO EXCHANGE! *THE MONK. THE MYSTERIES OF UDOLPHO.*

BETTER I WAS READING *VARNEY THE VAMPYR* AND *WAGNER THE WEHR-WOLF.*

OR *CHRISTABEL AND CARMILLA.*

WHAT?

NOTHING.

LADY'S KINSFOLK ARE IN THE HOUSE, ARE THEY NOT? HER BROTHER- AND SISTER-IN-LAW?

GEORGE AND SYLVIA, YES. BUT I AM THE HEAD OF THE HOUSEHOLD WHEN LADY IS... *INDISPOSED.*

MARIAH, YOU ARE NOT YET...WHAT? TWO-AND-TWENTY? DO THE OTHER SERVANTS KNOW OF LADY'S-- *CONDITION?*

THEY KNOW WHAT THEY *NEED* TO. LADY HAS ALWAYS HAD A WAY OF ATTACHING HERSELF TO PEOPLE EVEN MORE *HELPLESS* THAN HERSELF.

THE MEEK PROTECTING THE MEEK.

SHE IS NOT *MEEK* ANY LONGER.

YOU LOVE HER.

YES.

WILL YOU *PROTECT* HER AND HER CHILD? WILL YOU *KEEP HER SECRETS?*
ALWAYS, MARIAH--
MARIAH...?
WILLIAM... I NEVER WANTED YOU TO...IF I HAD EVER *H-HURT* YOU...
MY LADY...
WE MUST GO BACK. I CANNOT DO THIS BY MYSELF.
I CANNOT TRACK AS *YOU* CAN TRACK, MARIAH.
PLEASE.

Hampden Prison.
WILLIAM WILL PROTECT OUR SON FROM THAT VIPER WHILE WE ARE GONE.
AND YOU MUST BE CAREFUL, MY LADY. WE DO NOT KNOW WHAT TRIGGERED THE FIT.
I WOULD HAZARD THE WITCHERY HERE HAD SOMETHING TO DO WITH IT...
...THIS TOO IS THE HANDIWORK OF THE LONDON BUTCHER.
IT IS SO STRANGE, I HAVE BARELY HEARD A WORD OF THIS SPECTER, OR EVEN SEEN A PAPER IN THE HOUSE THAT MENTIONS HIS NAME... WHAT IS HE?
I DO NOT KNOW. BUT IF I AM TO TRACK THE BUTCHER DOWN, MY ABILITIES MUST BE...HEIGHTENED, TO PEER THROUGH ALL OF LONDON.
THIS IS MORE DANGEROUS THAN FINDING LITTLE HAKIM AFTER HE WAS STOLEN.
THE FORCE IT WILL TAKE...
MARIAH... I WILL GIVE YOU EXACTLY WHAT YOU NEED.

AHHH...
OHHH...
LIKE THIS...

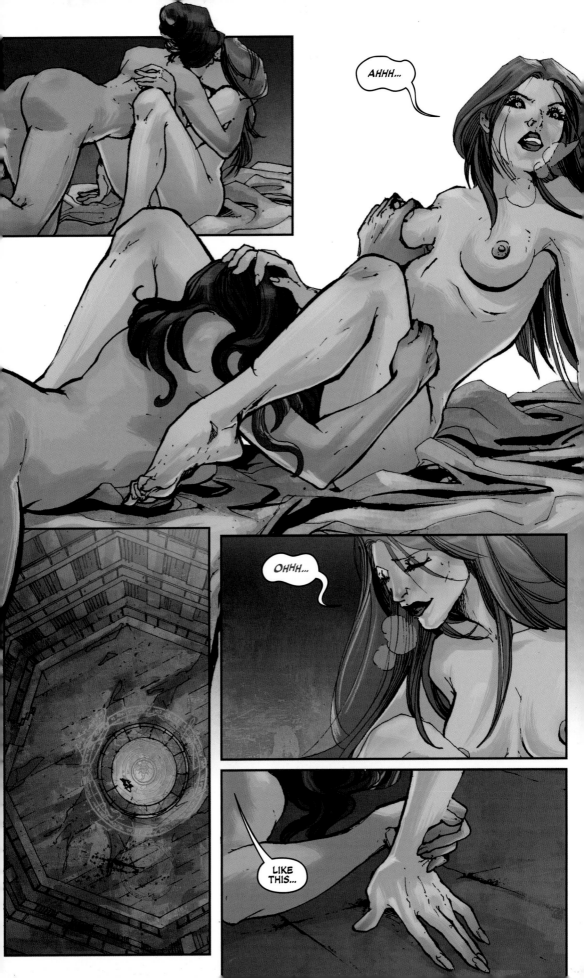

YES...
OH, YES...
LET ME LOOK AT YOU...
HERE, MY LOVE, GENTLY--
I HAVE SEEN HIM, MY DELIGHT...

Ahhh...
...I KNOW WHERE WE SHALL FIND HIM.

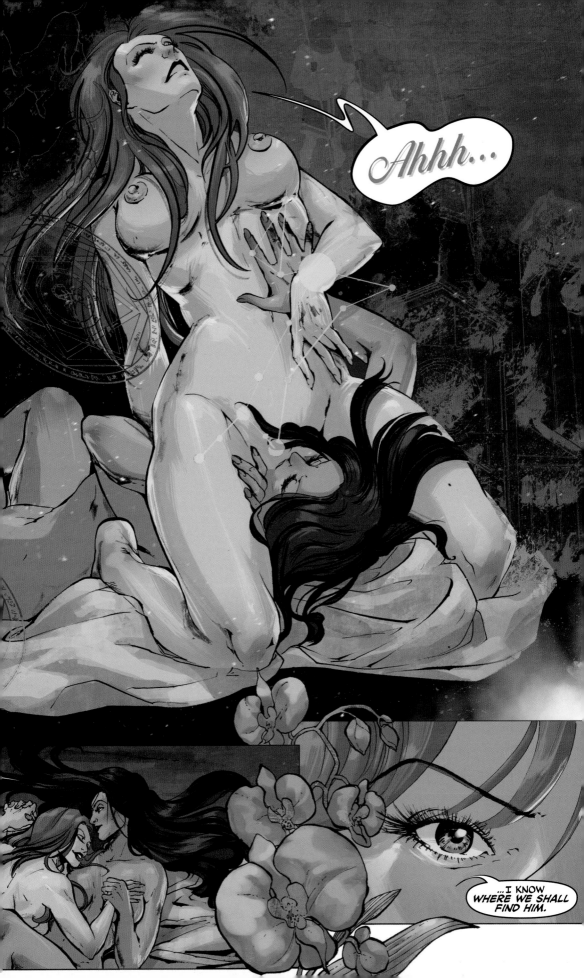

"THE LONDON BUTCHER IS MOVING, MY LADY.
"THIS IS NOT THE ACT OF A DESPERATE, HUNTED ANIMAL...
"HE IS ORDERLY. METHODICAL.
"HE CROSSES RIVERS REGULARLY, TO THROW US OFF HIS SCENT...
"SEE HOW HE MUDDLES HIS TRAIL? AND HE STOPS, ON THE CLOCK, AND LEAVES A SIGN?
"ALMOST AS IF HE IS CHECKING IN WITH OTHERS.
"HE IS NOT LIKE A SCAVENGER...
"HE IS LIKE A SOLDIER."
"THE MEAT MARKET, MARIAH?
"A PROPER HOME FOR A BUTCHER."
HAVE WE CAUGHT YOU AT YOUR MEAL?
ENJOY IT AS YOUR LAST.
IS THAT THE LORD'S TRUTH?

CAREFUL NOW, YOU NEWBORN *MONSTERS...*
...YOU ARE BUT A PASSING ABERRATION...
...MY KIND WAS HERE *LONG* BEFORE YOURS...
CRRRNCH
...AND WE WILL BE HERE WHEN YOU ARE *NO MORE.*

YOU SHALL ANSWER FOR YOUR CRIMES!
RRRG!
CRK

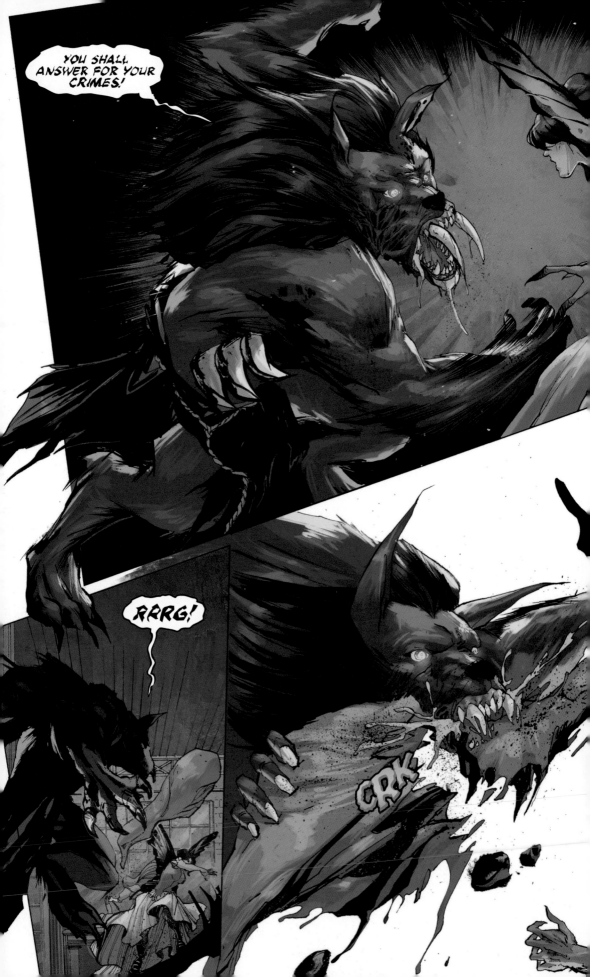

AHH!
MARIAH!
SHLK!

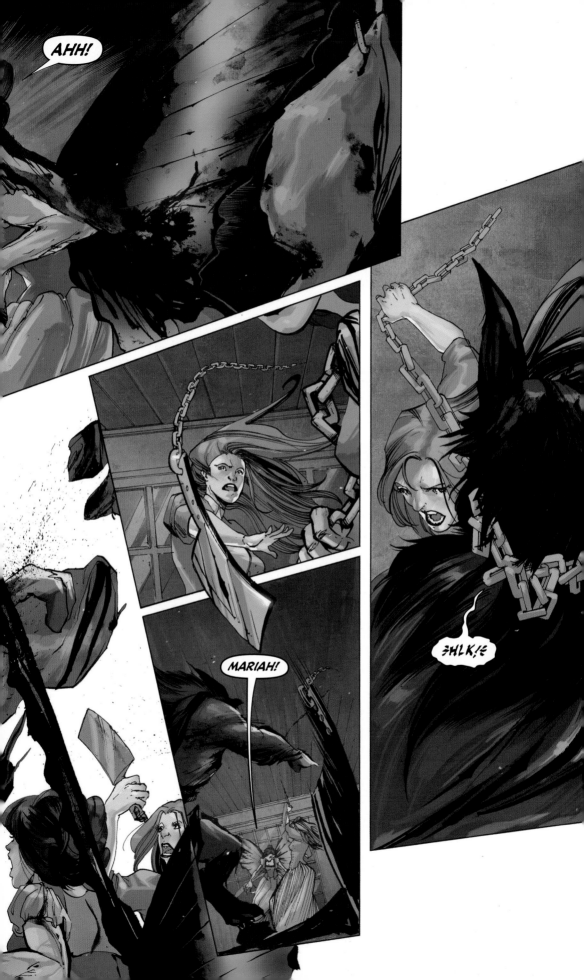

ONE MORE DEAD SINNER.
NEVER.
YOU WILL NEVER HURT MARIAH!
WHY DID YOU KILL ALL THOSE PEOPLE?! AND ALL THOSE PRISONERS?!
YOU'RE THE LONDON BUTCHER--
ANSWER ME!
AHHH!
I AM NOT THE LONDON BUTCHER, YOU BITCH--

YOU ARE.
HRAARGG!
CRN-SQUELCH
MARIAH!
WHAT HAVE WE DONE?

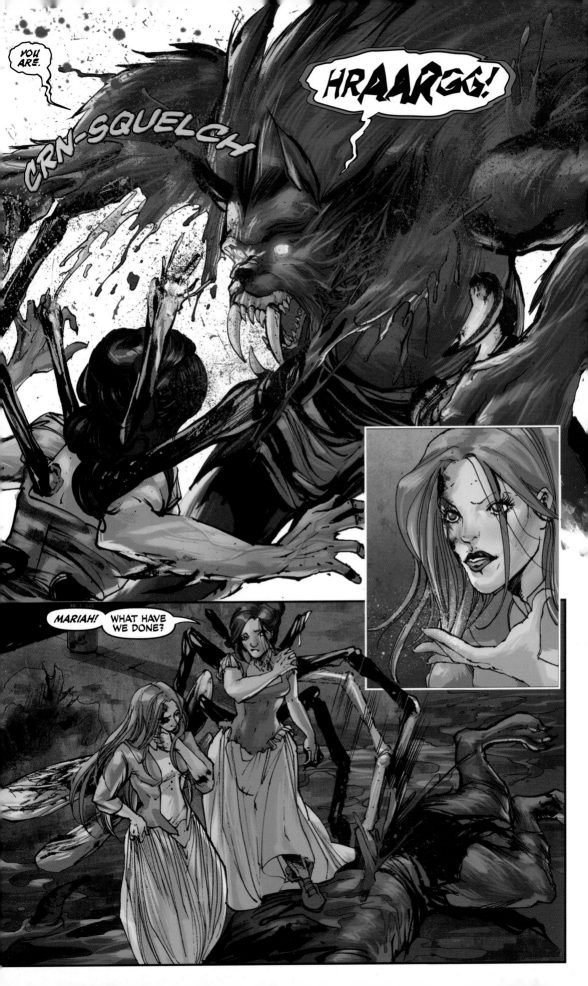

The Bertram Townhouse.

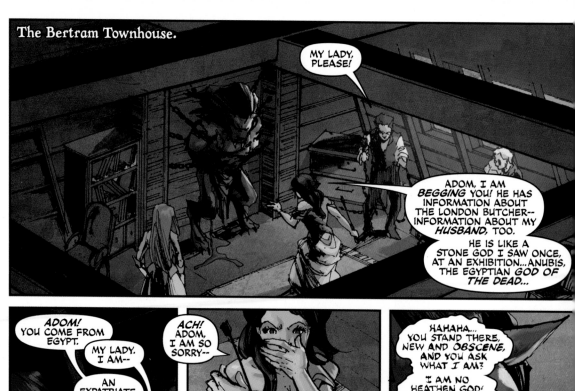

MY LADY, PLEASE!

ADOM, I AM *BEGGING* YOU! HE HAS INFORMATION ABOUT THE LONDON BUTCHER-- INFORMATION ABOUT MY *HUSBAND*, TOO.

HE IS LIKE A STONE GOD I SAW ONCE, AT AN EXHIBITION...ANUBIS, THE EGYPTIAN *GOD OF THE DEAD*...

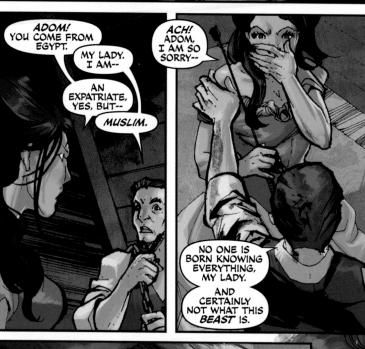

ADOM! YOU COME FROM EGYPT.

MY LADY, I AM--

AN *EXPATRIATE*, YES, BUT--

MUSLIM.

ACH! ADOM, I AM SO SORRY--

NO ONE IS BORN KNOWING EVERYTHING, MY LADY.

AND CERTAINLY NOT WHAT THIS *BEAST* IS.

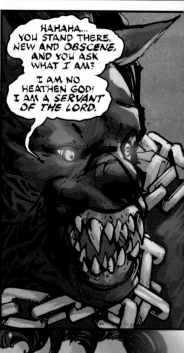

HAHAHA... YOU STAND THERE, NEW AND *OBSCENE*, AND YOU ASK WHAT *I* AM?

I AM NO HEATHEN GOD! I AM A *SERVANT OF THE LORD.*

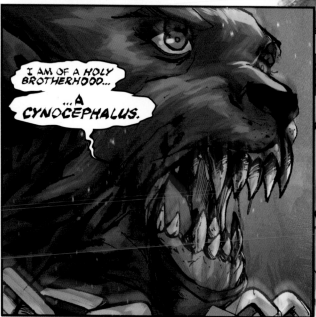

I AM OF A *HOLY BROTHERHOOD...*

...A *CYNOCEPHALUS.*

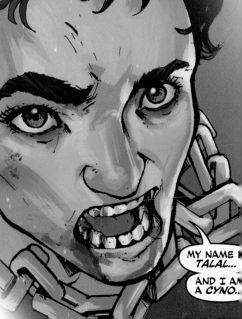

MY NAME [IS] TALAL...

AND I AM A CYNO...

"...MY BROTHERS AND I...
"...WE HAVE COME TO LONDON TO HUNT...
"...TO HUNT A CREATURE THAT ALREADY HUNTS AMONG YOU.
"IT IS OLD, AND PETTY, AND INSIDIOUS...
"...IT USES HOSTS TO DO ITS BIDDING...
"...IT FINDS THE WEAK, THE HATEFUL, THE SELF-LOATHING...
"...AND IT WORMS INTO THEIR HEARTS.
"WE CALL IT..."

"...THE HAG."
HA HA HA...
NEXT:
INSEXTS #5!

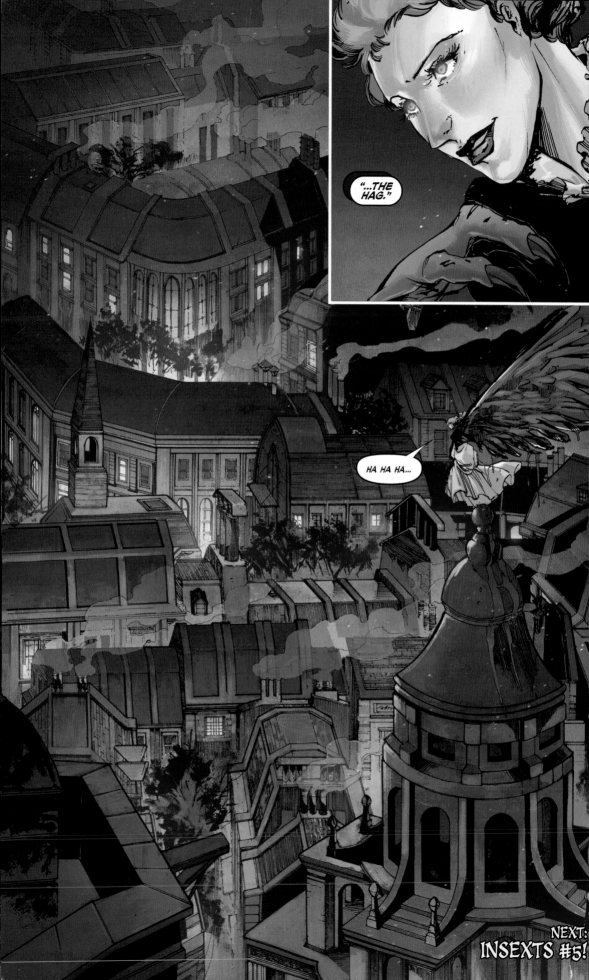

5

"CYNOCEPHALI"

The Attic of the Bertram Townhouse.
London. 1894.
I AM TALAL, A SERVANT OF THE LORD.
I AM OF THE ORDER OF CHRISTOPHER THE CYNOCEPHALUS...
...THE DOG-HEADED SOLDIER-SAINT.
I PERMITTED MYSELF TO BE SEIZED BY YOUR SCOTLAND YARD... CONFESSED TO YOUR CRIMES, THAT I MIGHT GAIN ACCESS TO THE IMPRISONED PREY I SOUGHT...
WHAT PREY? DEBTORS? PETTY THIEVES?!
NO.
MEN, WHO BOUGHT AND SOLD WOMEN, AND GIRLS, AND LITTLE CHILDREN...
...MEN, WHO SERVED YOUR HUSBAND.
MEN, WHO NO DOUBT SERVED YOU.
WELL, BUTCHER?!
I AM NOT AFRAID TO DIE!

GOOD.
I WILL NEED A KNIGHT IN SHINING ARMOR TO SEND TO HIS NOBLE DEATH SOON ENOUGH.
KRAK
I AM NOT WHAT YOU SEEK. I AM NO LONDON BUTCHER.
I HAVE KILLED, AND IF YOU WOULD TAKE MY HEAD FOR KILLING VIOLATORS OF WOMEN AND LITTLE CHILDREN--
--THEN I WILL CUT YOUR HEART OUT HERE AND LET YOU BLEED OUT AS I EAT IT.
NO...NO! IS IT NO LIE?!
I CAN SMELL NOTHING ON YOU, NO DECEIT, NO...
...HOW CAN THIS BE?!
I HAVE SLAIN VILE SOULS IN THIS CITY.
AND I HAVE SEEN YOU DO THE SAME.
BUT THERE ARE DEAD WOMEN AND GIRLS AND CHILDREN FOR WHOM NEITHER OF US CAN ACCOUNT.
MY LADY...

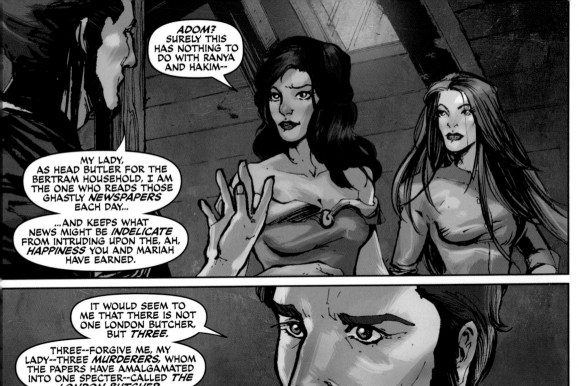

ADOM? SURELY THIS HAS NOTHING TO DO WITH RANYA AND HAKIM--

MY LADY, AS HEAD BUTLER FOR THE BERTRAM HOUSEHOLD, I AM THE ONE WHO READS THOSE GHASTLY *NEWSPAPERS* EACH DAY...

...AND KEEPS WHAT NEWS MIGHT BE *INDELICATE* FROM INTRUDING UPON THE, AH, *HAPPINESS* YOU AND MARIAH HAVE EARNED.

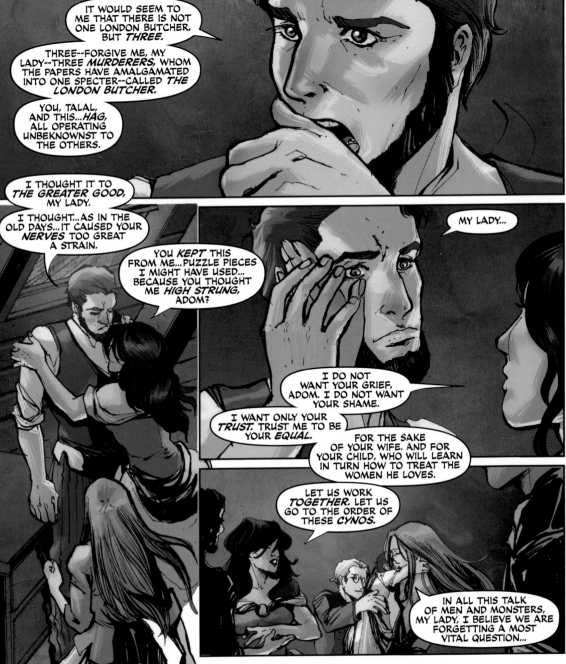

IT WOULD SEEM TO ME THAT THERE IS NOT ONE LONDON BUTCHER, BUT *THREE.*

THREE--FORGIVE ME, MY LADY--THREE *MURDERERS,* WHOM THE PAPERS HAVE AMALGAMATED INTO ONE SPECTER--CALLED *THE LONDON BUTCHER.*

YOU, TALAL, AND THIS...*HAG,* ALL OPERATING UNBEKNOWNST TO THE OTHERS.

I THOUGHT IT TO *THE GREATER GOOD,* MY LADY.

I THOUGHT...AS IN THE OLD DAYS...IT CAUSED YOUR *NERVES* TOO GREAT A STRAIN.

YOU *KEPT* THIS FROM ME...PUZZLE PIECES I MIGHT HAVE USED... BECAUSE YOU THOUGHT ME *HIGH STRUNG,* ADOM?

MY LADY...

I DO NOT WANT YOUR GRIEF, ADOM. I DO NOT WANT YOUR SHAME.

I WANT ONLY YOUR *TRUST.* TRUST ME TO BE YOUR *EQUAL.*

FOR THE SAKE OF YOUR WIFE. AND FOR YOUR CHILD, WHO WILL LEARN IN TURN HOW TO TREAT THE WOMEN HE LOVES.

LET US WORK *TOGETHER.* LET US GO TO THE ORDER OF THESE *CYNOS.*

IN ALL THIS TALK OF MEN AND MONSTERS, MY LADY, I BELIEVE WE ARE FORGETTING A MOST VITAL QUESTION...

The House of Madame H.
"...WHERE ARE THE WOMEN THAT YOUR HUSBAND BOUGHT AND SOLD?"
MY NAME IS LORD GEORGE BERTRAM.
I DISCOVERED THE ADDRESS TO YOUR... ESTABLISHMENT... AMID MY LATE BROTHER'S POSSESSIONS.
YOU MIGHT DO A SERVICE TO YOUR BETTERS, TO AN OLD FAMILY, FOR WHICH WE WOULD NOT BE UNGRATEFUL.
I TAKE IT YOU ARE THE MADAM HERE?
...

...?
I--I BELIEVE MY BROTHER'S WIDOW HAS BEEN-- *UNFAITHFUL* TO HIM.
HE... *FAVORED* A GIRL HERE, FOR HER, AH, *INITIAL VIRTUE*...
ELSIE.
SHE WAS A *MAIDEN* WHEN HE BOUGHT HER.
PLEASE... CAN'T I JUST GO BACK TO MY--
SHH, ELSIE, DON'T MAKE IT *WORSE.*
SOON ENOUGH, YOU'LL SEE IF HIS *BASTARD* MATCHES THE ONE IN *YOUR BROTHER'S HOUSE.*
AH!
I DID NOT SEE YOU MOVE, I--
I MEAN, YES. SHE IS--ONLY A FEW WEEKS MORE, I MEAN...
THEN WE SHALL HAVE WHAT *PROOF* WE NEED TO THROW THAT HARLOT FROM THE HOUSE...
TELL ME, GEORGE BERTRAM...
...*WHY DO YOU CARE?*

?!
YOU ARE AFRAID THEY ARE LAUGHING AT YOU-- ALL THOSE PRETTY GIRLS, RICH GIRLS, PEASANT GIRLS WITH NOTHING BUT DIRT IN THEIR VEINS.
THAT IS WHY YOU CHOSE A WOMAN WHO DOES NOT LAUGH, DOES NOT EVEN CRY.
A WOMAN WHOSE HATRED OF WOMEN EXCEEDS EVEN YOUR OWN.
YOU COULD ATTRACT NO PRETTY HEIRESS. AND YOU REFUSED THE UGLY ONES WHO WOULD HAVE YOU. OHHH, NOT YOU-- YOU DESERVED BETTER.
AND THE BRIDE YOU CHOSE-- BROKEN AS SHE IS-- WAS BETTER THAN A CREATURE WHOLE AND UNTAMED.
YOU DESPISED THAT YOUR FAMILY HAD TO BE SAVED BY A YOUNGER BROTHER'S TIMELY MARRIAGE...
...TO A BROWN, BLOWN, BLOWSY CREATURE WHO HAS FOUND A WAY TO BE HAPPIER THAN YOU HAVE EVER KNOWN.
AHHH!
YOU HAVE NEVER SAVED THE THINGS YOU WANTED TO LOVE AND WHICH YOU WANTED TO LOVE YOU.
BUT THAT HALF-BREED WENCH HAD MORE POWER AND JOY THAN YOU COULD EVER DREAM.
YOU--AND NOT YOUR BROTHER-- SHOULD'VE BEEN THE ONE TO DIE!
⇒PANT⇐ HOW--HOW COULD YOU KNOW?!
I AM THE HAG!
I AM DRAWN TO HATEFUL THINGS...
...SWEET AND ROTTEN AS FRUIT DROPPED IN THE ORCHARD...
...AS THE FLIES AND WASPS AND CREEPING THINGS COME TO MATE AND SWARM.

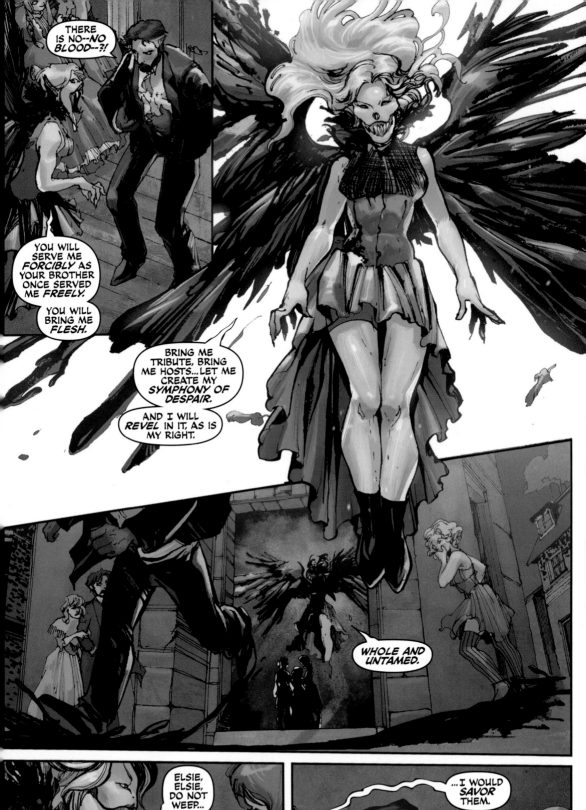

THERE IS NO--*NO BLOOD*--?!

YOU WILL SERVE ME *FORCIBLY* AS YOUR BROTHER ONCE SERVED ME *FREELY.*

YOU WILL BRING ME *FLESH.*

BRING ME TRIBUTE, BRING ME HOSTS...LET ME CREATE MY *SYMPHONY OF DESPAIR.*

AND I WILL *REVEL* IN IT, AS IS MY RIGHT.

WHOLE AND UNTAMED.

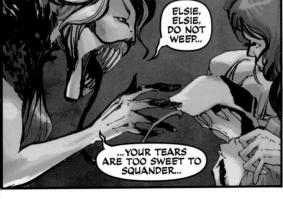

ELSIE, ELSIE, DO NOT WEEP...

...YOUR TEARS ARE TOO SWEET TO SQUANDER...

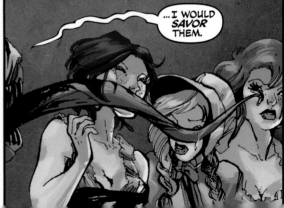

...I WOULD *SAVOR* THEM.

The Church of St. Christopher.
HURRY, MY LADIES!
WILLIAM, ADOM AND RANYA WILL KEEP HAKIM AND OUR SON SAFE, SURELY?
WE MUST FIND A WAY TO DEAL WITH SYLVIA--
CASTING SYLVIA AND GEORGE OUT OF THE HOUSE WOULD INVITE SCANDAL AND PRYING EYES...
...OUR LIVES WOULD NOT PRESENTLY HOLD UP TO SCRUTINY, MY HEART...
"...AND I FEAR THERE ARE STILL MORE SECRETS TO COME."

BROTHER TALAL...YOU BRING A VILLAINESS INTO THE HOLY ORDER OF THE CYNOCEPHALI?!
BROTHER ASHER! THESE ARE TRULY GREAT LADIES.
BROTHER ASHER. I AM LADY. THIS IS MY BELOVED, MARIAH.
WE ARE PREPARED TO OFFER OUR ASSISTANCE TO YOUR ORDER IN DESTROYING THIS HAG AND RESCUING THOSE SHE HAS ENSLAVED.
SNIFF
YOU ARE NO LADIES.
YOU ARE SOMETHING NEW.
I KNOW YOUR SCENT, AS SURELY AS YOU KNOW MINE, BROTHER ASHER.
THOUGH TALAL OBEYS YOUR COMMAND, IT IS A TRACE OF YOU AND NOT HIM THAT I DETECTED IN THE WITCHERY ON THE FLOOR OF HAMPDEN PRISON.
WITCHERY, HA. I GAVE TALAL THE SPELL TO PAINT THE TRAP OF SOLOMON.
I BELIEVED THE HAG WOULD COME TO ITS SUMMONS...SHE IS DRAWN TO SUFFERING AS A BEE TO POLLEN.
INSTEAD, I WAS THE ONE WHO TRIGGERED ITS CURSE.
YET IT DID NOT KILL YOU.
NO. IT SICKENED ME.
A CURE FOR A SICKNESS YOU DID NOT HAVE.
SUCH CURES HAVE KILLED INNOCENT WOMEN BEFORE.

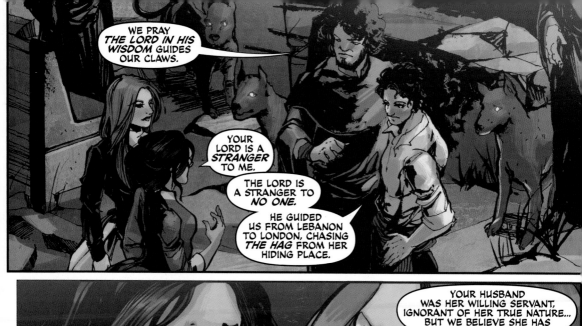

WE PRAY *THE LORD IN HIS WISDOM* GUIDES OUR CLAWS.

YOUR LORD IS A *STRANGER* TO ME.

THE LORD IS A STRANGER TO *NO ONE.*

HE GUIDED US FROM LEBANON TO LONDON, CHASING *THE HAG* FROM HER HIDING PLACE.

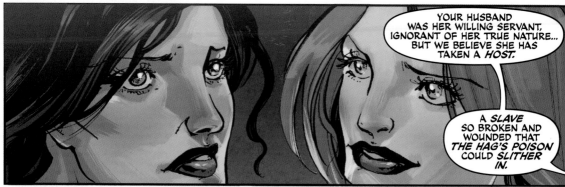

YOUR HUSBAND WAS HER WILLING SERVANT, IGNORANT OF HER TRUE NATURE... BUT WE BELIEVE SHE HAS TAKEN A *HOST.*

A *SLAVE* SO BROKEN AND WOUNDED THAT *THE HAG'S POISON* COULD *SLITHER IN.*

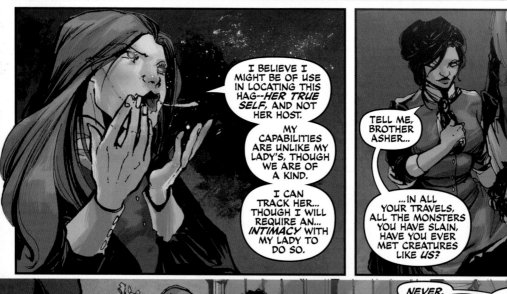

I BELIEVE I MIGHT BE OF USE IN LOCATING THIS HAG--*HER TRUE SELF,* AND NOT HER HOST.

MY CAPABILITIES ARE UNLIKE MY LADY'S, THOUGH WE ARE OF A KIND.

I CAN TRACK HER... THOUGH I WILL REQUIRE AN... *INTIMACY* WITH MY LADY TO DO SO.

TELL ME, BROTHER ASHER...

...IN ALL YOUR TRAVELS, ALL THE MONSTERS YOU HAVE SLAIN, HAVE YOU EVER MET CREATURES LIKE *US?*

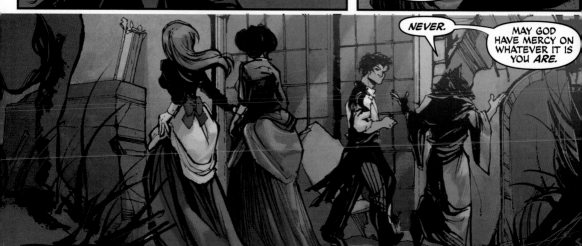

NEVER.

MAY GOD HAVE MERCY ON WHATEVER IT IS YOU *ARE.*

YESSSS, MY LOVE...
MY LOVE...?
NO-- DO NOT STOP, I CAN DO THIS--
MARIAH, NEVER.
PLEASE. SPEAK TO ME...
I KEEP THINKING OF WILLIAM... I KNOW IT WAS I WHO URGED YOU TO CONFIDE IN HIM, BUT HE LOVES YOU SO TRULY, MY LADY...
...HE KNOWS THE SECRET OF YOUR BODY, BUT NOT THE SECRET OF YOUR HEART.
I THINK AGAIN AND AGAIN HOW MUCH SAFER YOU WOULD BE-- WE WOULD BE--IF YOU TOOK ANOTHER HUSBAND.
WE WOULD HAVE A VOICE IN SOCIETY, A PROTECTOR...
YOU HAVE ALWAYS BEEN THE ONLY PROTECTOR I NEED.

"YOU AND OUR CHILD ARE THE *TRUEST LOVE* IN MY HEART."
The House of Madame H.
YES.
AHH AHHH
HURT EACH OTHER.

?
WHO... SPIES...?!
The Bertram Townhouse.
AHH!
YES, MISTRESS.
I LISTEN.
I OBEY.

"AND THE WOODSMAN TOOK AN AXE, AND SNUCK UP ON THE SLEEPING WOLF..."
SYLVIA! IT'S SYLVIA!
"LADY, SHE'S GOING TO KILL OUR SON!"

The Bertram Townhouse.
WILL!
ADOM! RANYA!
MY LADY!
LYE FOR THE LIES YOU SPREAD, COUNTESS.
HISSSS
WHORES AND VERMIN, UNFAITHFUL AND UNCHASTE!
SLATTERNS, STRUMPETS AND DRIED-UP OLD SPINSTERS WHO LOVED PRIDE MORE THAN DUTY--
--BROODMARES IN RUT, WITH SQUALLING CLUTCHES OF SNOT-FACED BRATS--
--COWS AND CUNTS WHO THINK THEMSELVES QUEENS--

AHHH!
LEARN. YOUR. PLACE.
HARLOTS, HAGS, AND WHORES-- NAGS AND SOWS AND SHREWS!
STUPID-- LYING--MAD-- NEEDFUL BITCH--
OH, SISTER...

...STILL YOUR TONGUE.

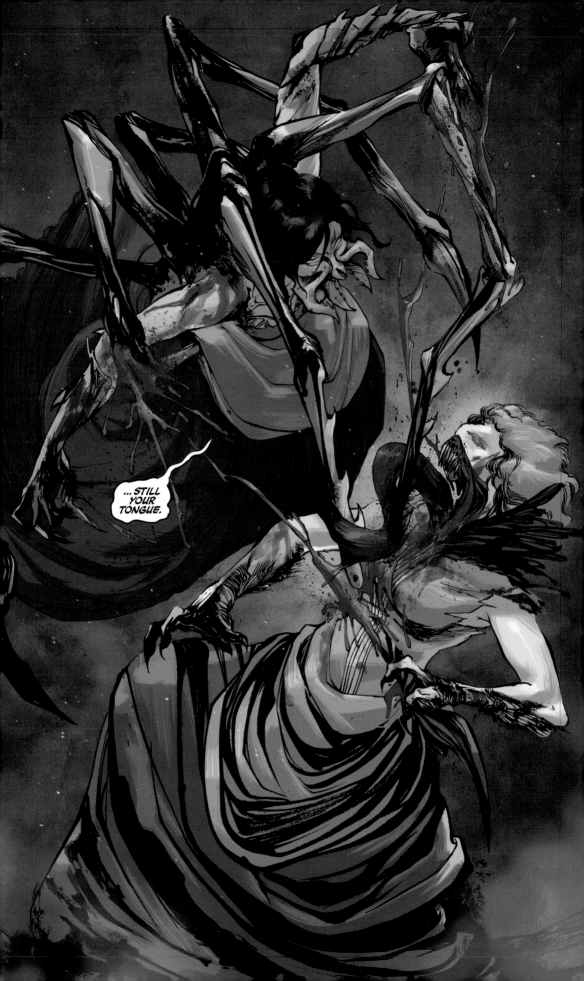

CHITTER CHITTER CHITTER
L-LADY--

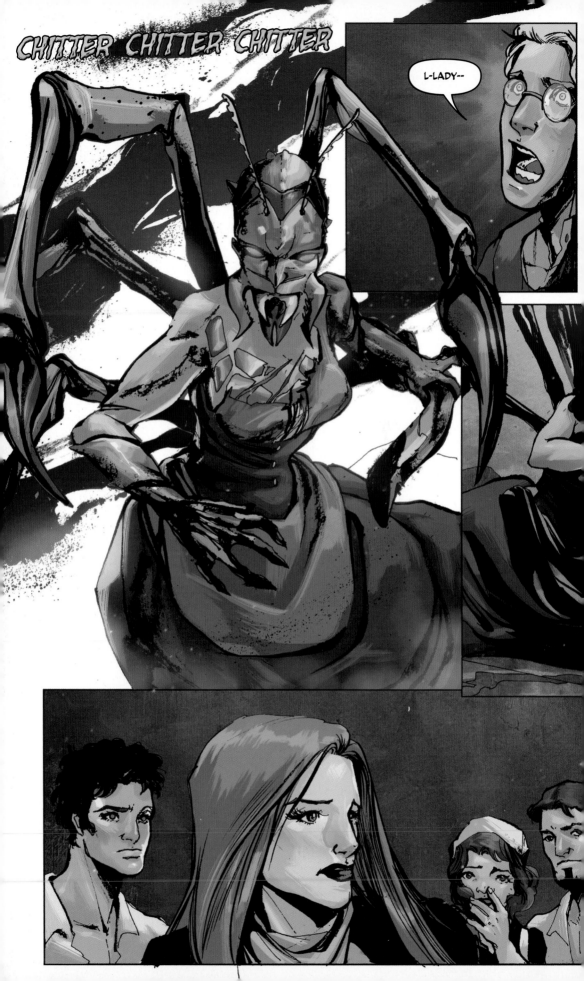

CHT
CHT
CHT
MY LOVE.
MY LIFE.
COME BACK TO ME.
...
WE MUST BURN THE CORPSE.

AND THEN WE WILL BURN THE HAG...
...AND ALL HER SERVANTS...
...TO THE GROUND.
NEXT: INSEXTS CHAPTER VI

6

"BORDELLO"

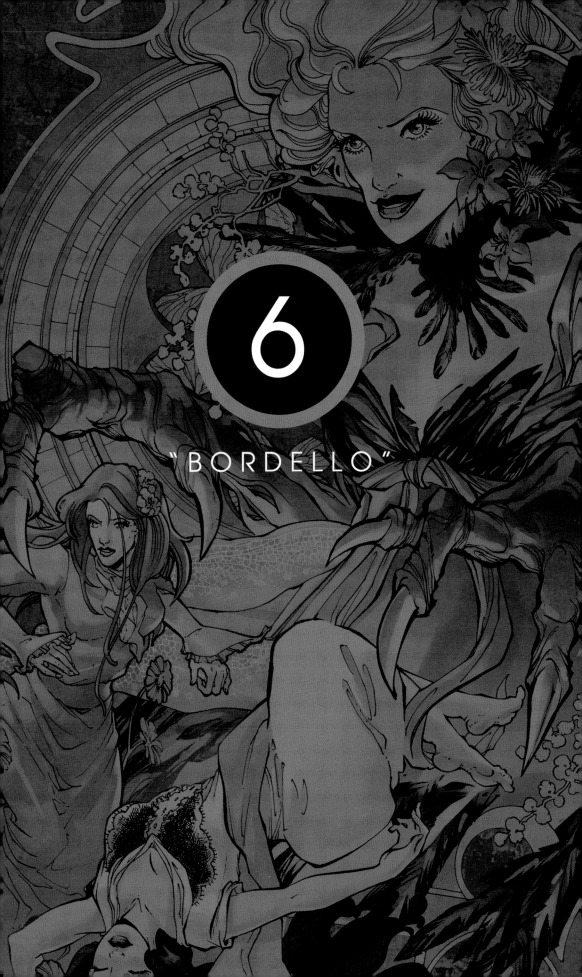

Night.
LADY...?
...LADY LALITA BERTRAM?
LISTEN TO ME, LALITA BERTRAM...
...LISTEN TO ME...
...OR I WILL EAT YOUR LOVER IN FRONT OF YOU...
...AND YOU WILL LAP UP FROM THE FLOOR WHATEVER PUS AND SLUDGE REMAINS.
ARE YOU PAYING ATTENTION, LALITA BERTRAM?
HOW YOU HATE THE SOUND OF YOUR OWN NAME.
THE FIRST FOR THE SHAME OF YOUR BLOOD AND BIRTH...
...AND THE LATTER SHACKLES YOU CHOSE.
THE ONLY NAME THAT MADE YOU HAPPY WAS THE NAME THEY GAVE YOU.
LADY... LADY...
...MY LADY.
TELL ME, LALITA BERTRAM...
...HOW DO THEY TASTE?

Three Days Before.
The Bertram Household.
GEORGE HASN'T RETURNED YET...
...HE DOESN'T KNOW HIS WIFE IS DEAD.
SYLVIA'S BODY WENT MISSING IN THE NIGHT...
...MY LADY, I DO NOT LIKE THIS.
I DO NOT LIKE THESE CYNOS.
WE NEED BROTHER ASHER'S MAGIC TO HIDE US FROM THE HAG, WILLIAM.
EVEN MARIAH, IN HER VISION, FELT THE CREATURE'S EYES UPON HER.
MY LADY...I CAN PROTECT YOU FROM SCANDAL. I CAN PROTECT YOU FROM POVERTY. I CAN PROTECT YOU, EVEN, FROM THE LAWS OF THE LAND...
...BUT I CANNOT PROTECT YOU FROM THIS.
WE COULD TURN BACK.
NO, WILLIAM.
YOU ARE MY FRIEND, AND I LOVE YOU... BUT NO.
ONCE THE BUTTERFLY IS FREE...
...IT DOES NOT GO BACK INTO THE CHRYSALIS.
THE INSECT FLIES...

The House of Madame H.
"...OR THE INSECT DIES."

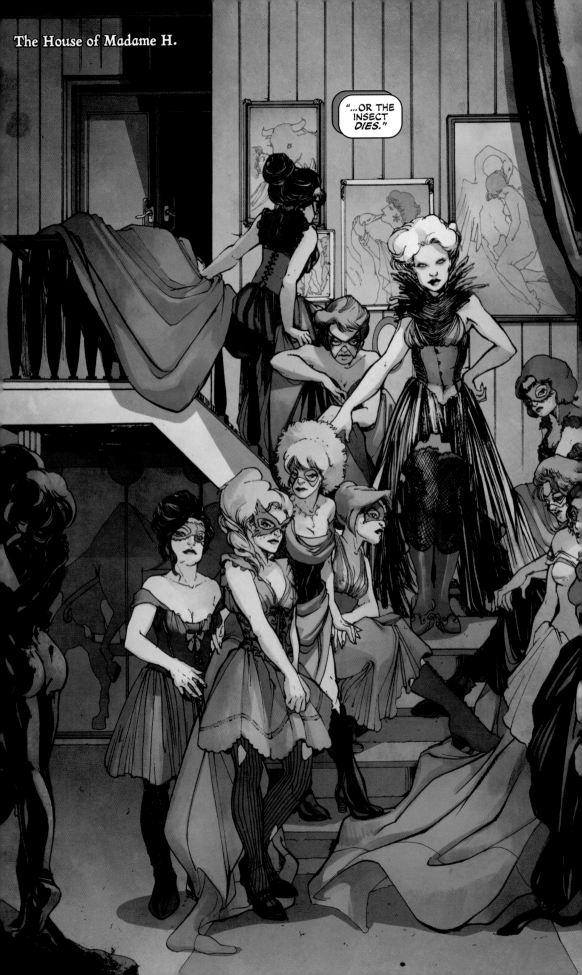

MADAME!
HAHA, I AM-- *HIC* -- I AM SIR JOHN GREELEY, AND THIS IS THE MISTRESS OF MY HEART.
WE ARE FRESH TO LONDON AND LOOKING TO RENT, NOT BUY--IF YOU FOLLOW MY STEP.
RENT.
WHICH?
W-WHY--WHY, RENT THE WHOLE HOUSE!
WE ARE LOOKING FOR RATHER... RARIFIED PLEASURES. I WAS TOLD YOUR HOUSE WAS THE ONLY ONE THAT MIGHT OFFER THEM.
AND THAT IF YOU DO NOT HAVE AMONG YOUR WARES WHAT A CUSTOMER MIGHT SEEK, YOU ARE ABLE TO... ACQUIRE STOCK AT MARKET.
I'LL SEE THE COLOR OF YOUR MONEY OR THE COLOR OF YOUR GUTS, LITTLE LORD.
USHER THEM UPSTAIRS.
WE CAN WORK TO YOUR OWN IMAGINATION, SIR GREELEY.
PERHAPS YOU WOULD SEE YOUR MISTRESS DRAPED AS ISHTAR AND YOU AS HER BA'AL, IN A HAREM OF WORSHIPPING SLAVES?
PERHAPS YOU WOULD SEE YOUR APPETITE FOR THE EXOTIC FILLED WITH GIRLS FROM FARTHER EAST THAN SHE, TO DISCIPLINE AND BRING TO GOD?
OR PERHAPS, IF YOUR TASTES ARE SO RARIFIED...
...YOU WOULD LIKE TO SEE YOUR HUNTING HOUNDS PERFORM WITH SOME OF OUR PUSSYCATS?

YOUR ROOM, MISSUS -- I--
MISSUS, SO SORRY, BUT AM I KNOWIN' YOU?
YES, HATTIE, IT'S ME--
THE LADY! THE LADY WHO RESCUED US FROM THE BEASTIE--
HERE TO RESCUE YOU FROM MORE THAN THAT.
HERE, SIT, YOU POOR THING--
I LIKE-- SNIFF -- I LIKE YOUR DOG.
I ALWAYS LIKED DOGS.
MAY I PET HIM?
ONLY IF HE'LL BE A GENTLEMAN ABOUT IT.
!
YOUR CAPTOR IS NOT THE ONLY ONE WITH MAGIC.
VHIIIISH
HATTIE, THIS IS TALAL. HE IS A CYNO, AND SWORN TO AID YOU.
IT'S A FUNNY WORLD WHEN MUTTS TURNING INTO LADS DON'T MAKE ME TWITCH AN EYE.
I'VE SEEN TOO MUCH CHANGE ALREADY.

"IT WASN'T LIKE THIS BEFORE, MISSUS.
"SOME HERE, AYE, THEY STARTED BECAUSE THEY WAS GOIN' HUNGRY...
"...BECAUSE THEIR PARENTS BEAT THEM, BECAUSE SOME LORDLING DONE THEM WRONG, HURT THEM, RUINED THEM...
"BUT ME..."
...AND WE WHO LIVE TO SUFFER AS SEASONS FLAME AND DIE KNOW THE HOPE OF EVERY CREEPING THING TO BE A BUTTERFLY!
"...I LIKED IT.
"I SANG IN A TAVERN, AND THE BOYS, THE GOOD BOYS, THEY WERE SO SWEET.
"AND THERE WAS NO HARM IN A BIT OF JOY ON A COLD NIGHT, AND IF THAT JOY PUT A ROOF OVER MY HEAD, OH...
"AND THEN SHE CAME.
"WE DIDN'T KNOW HER FOR WHAT SHE WAS, AT FIRST...
"...AT FIRST, INDEED, WE LOVED HER.
"WHEN SHE MADE US FEEL ASHAMED, WE WANTED TO PLEASE HER.
"WHEN SHE MADE US FEEL WANTED, THERE WAS NO PLEASURE GREATER.
"SHE SPOKE OF GOOD GIRLS, OF LADIES, OF THE THINGS SHE ESTEEMED AND WE STRUGGLED TO BE THEM...

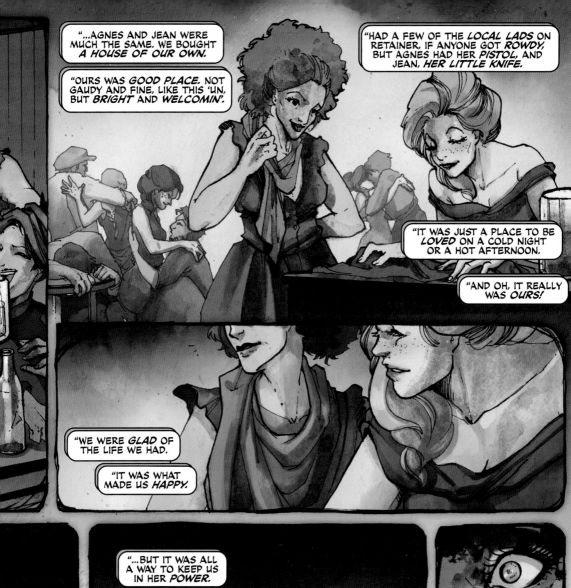

"...AGNES AND JEAN WERE MUCH THE SAME. WE BOUGHT *A HOUSE OF OUR OWN.*

"OURS WAS *GOOD PLACE.* NOT GAUDY AND FINE, LIKE THIS 'UN, BUT *BRIGHT* AND *WELCOMIN'.*

"HAD A FEW OF THE *LOCAL LADS* ON RETAINER, IF ANYONE GOT *ROWDY,* BUT AGNES HAD HER *PISTOL,* AND JEAN, *HER LITTLE KNIFE.*

"IT WAS JUST A PLACE TO BE *LOVED* ON A COLD NIGHT OR A HOT AFTERNOON.

"AND OH, IT REALLY WAS *OURS!*

"WE WERE *GLAD* OF THE LIFE WE HAD.

"IT WAS WHAT MADE US *HAPPY.*

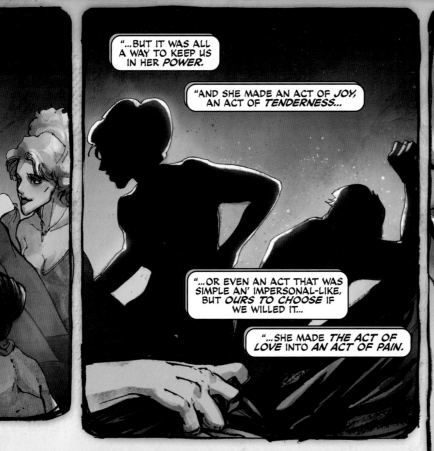
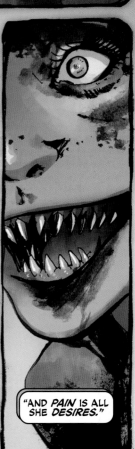

"...BUT IT WAS ALL A WAY TO KEEP US IN HER *POWER.*

"AND SHE MADE AN ACT OF *JOY,* AN ACT OF *TENDERNESS...*

"...OR EVEN AN ACT THAT WAS SIMPLE AN' IMPERSONAL-LIKE, BUT *OURS TO CHOOSE* IF WE WILLED IT...

"...SHE MADE *THE ACT OF LOVE* INTO *AN ACT OF PAIN.*

"AND *PAIN* IS ALL SHE *DESIRES.*"

"SHE GROWS FAT AS A TICK ON BLOOD WHEN SHE FEELS ANOTHER CREATURE SUFFER BENEATH HER.
"AND WHY?
"I'M SURE THERE'S A TALE TO HER, TOO.
"BEATEN AND BROKEN BY THE SCEPTER THAT RULES THE WORLD.
LA MALINCHE!
CHINGADA!
"CRUSHED BY THE RULE THAT MAKES US DEVOUR EACH OTHER...
"...INSTEAD OF MAKING COMMON CAUSE AGAINST THE REIGN...
"...THAT MAKES US HURT EACH OTHER SO.
"PERHAPS SHE WAS WILLING TO KNEEL TO THE ORDER OF THE WORLD...
"...TO PLAY A BRUTAL GAME...
"...SO LONG AS IT MEANT SHE WAS ON THE WINNING SIDE.
"BUT WHATEVER MADE HER DOESN'T MATTER.
"SHE CHOSE WHAT TO DO WITH THE POWER SHE GAINED.
"AND SHE CHOSE TO HURT US...
"...BUT WE WILL NOT CHOOSE TO DIE."

BROTHER TALAL.
WE BORE YOUR PLAN TO BRING US INTO THIS HELL.
IT HAS BEEN TWO DAYS, AND YOUR MONSTROUS ALLY HAS FLITTED AND FLIRTED AND PRETENDED TO GO THROUGH TEN CASKS OF CHAMPAGNE--
--YET WE ARE NO CLOSER TO THE HAG'S HEAD ON A SPIKE.
BROTHER ASHER! WE HAVE DONE SUCH GOOD, THOUGH-- ARMED THE WOMEN OF THIS DEN--
--TO EACH MAIDEN, A CYNO.
TO EACH MAIDEN, A WEAPON.
"MAIDEN"?
GRAH! THIS PLACE REEKS OF SIN.
AND THE HAG'S SERVANTS MAY TURN ON US AT ANY MOMENT, JUST AS THE COUNTESS DID WHEN HER MISTRESS BID.
THESE WOMEN ARE NOT HER WILLING SERVANTS. THEY ARE NOT LIKE LADY'S HUSBAND, WHO SERVED THE HAG FREELY.
I QUESTION YOUR LOYALTY, TALAL.
WE HAVE A MISSION OF OUR OWN.
"WE HAVE BEEN CHOSEN BY THE FATHER ALMIGHTY TO PURGE EVIL AND SIN FROM THE WORLD."

Day One.
"WE ARE EXPECTED TO ENJOY WHAT SHE OFFERS."
RABBIT FUR.
Day Two.
A HUNT.
"NO...
"...A HAREM.
"SOME THINGS, I CANNOT PREVENT.
"THOSE THINGS, I WILL AVENGE."

...y Three.
YES, DANCING!
IS HARDLY SOMETHING YOU COULD NOT FIND IN LONDON.
FOR THE RATES YOU ARE PAYING--
FOR THE RATES I AM PAYING, I WISH TO SEE DANCING!
I PROPOSE A NEW AMUSEMENT.
THE LAST SHIPMENT I EVER HAD, BEFORE MY ERSTWHILE SERVANT WOUND UP DROWNED IN THE THAMES...
...THEY UNDERSTAND PRECIOUS LITTLE ENGLISH.
THEY WILL NOT UNDERSTAND WHY YOU ARE DOING THIS TO THEM.
ENOUGH.
OH YES, I DO AGREE...
ENOUGH.

YOU HAVE YOUR *CHARMS,* WOMAN.
CHARMS NOT KNOWN, I THINK, TO *ALL* WOMEN.
KILL THEM, MY BEAUTIES.
KILL THESE *DOGS.*
YOU WOULD PUT YOUR FAITH IN *BEASTS* THAT CALL THEMSELVES *MEN OF GOD?*
EVEN IF THEY SAVE YOU, WILL YOU BE *SLAVE-NUNS,* SHUT UP IN *THE TOMB OF AN ABBEY?*
DRUDGES IN FACTORIES, FROSTBITTEN AND DESPISED--OR FREE AND FALLEN WOMEN, BANISHED TO *SLUMS?*
TO WHOM SHALL YOU APPEAL?
NO ONE WOULD *PITY* YOU.
NO ONE WOULD *LOVE* YOU.

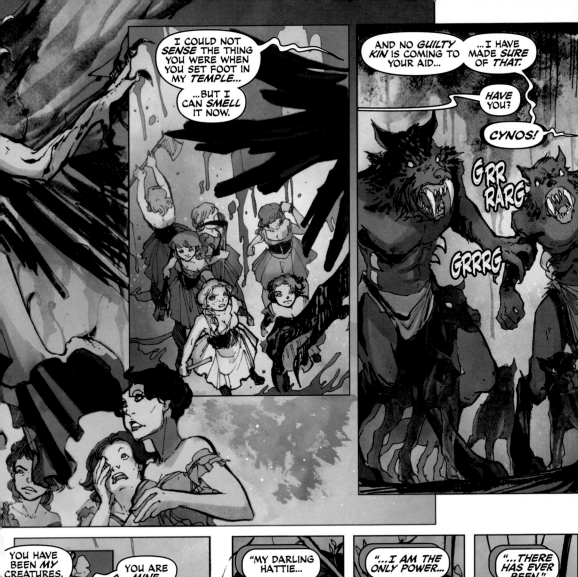

I COULD NOT *SENSE* THE THING YOU WERE WHEN YOU SET FOOT IN MY *TEMPLE*...

...BUT I CAN *SMELL* IT NOW.

AND NO *GUILTY KIN* IS COMING TO YOUR AID...

...I HAVE MADE *SURE* OF *THAT*.

HAVE YOU?

CYNOS!

GRR RARG

GRRRG

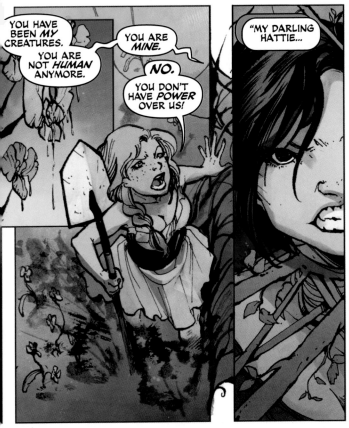

YOU HAVE BEEN *MY* CREATURES.

YOU ARE *MINE*.

YOU ARE NOT *HUMAN* ANYMORE.

NO.

YOU DON'T HAVE *POWER* OVER US!

"MY DARLING HATTIE...

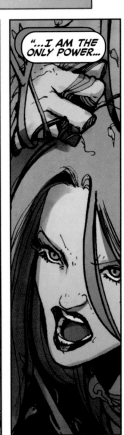

"...I AM THE *ONLY* POWER...

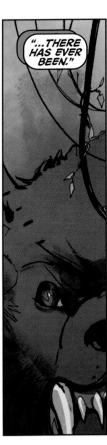

"...THERE *HAS* EVER BEEN."

THERE IS SUCH WONDER AND GRACE IN WOMEN.
UNLESS THEY CAN BE TAUGHT TO HATE THEMSELVES AND EACH OTHER...
...THEY MIGHT OVERRUN THE EARTH.
HATRED OF WOMEN IS THE OLDEST LAW THERE HAS EVER BEEN.
FORTUNATELY, IT IS A LAW YOUR KIND CAN BE TRAINED TO OBEY.
BUT IF IT IS POWER YOU WANT, THEN I WILL BESTOW IT ON YOU.
REVENGE YOURSELVES UPON THE MEN WHO HAVE HARMED YOU, WHO HAVE DRIVEN YOU INTO THE GUTTER WITH THEIR CROSSES AND HYMNS.
REVENGE YOURSELVES UPON THE WOMEN WHO PRESUME TO SAVE YOU, WHO SNEER AT YOUR CHOICES, WHO THINK THEMSELVES BETTER.
BE THE REVENGE WE ALL COULD NOT TAKE...
...AND I WILL BREAK OPEN THE MARROW OF THEIR VERY BONES.
NO.
"NO"...?

NO.
YER A *LIAR,* MISTRESS.
YOU WANT US *TO HATE EACH OTHER* SO WE'RE TOO *WORN DOWN* TO *HATE YOU.*
YOU SAY WHAT YOU THINK WE WANT TO *HEAR,* SO LONG WE'RE STILL DOIN' WHAT IT IS *YOU* SAY.
YOU PREACH AS IF YER *HATE,* YER *WAY,* IS *THE ONLY GAME IN TOWN.*
WELL--
SSSSSSSSSS
--WE AIN'T *PLAYIN'* ANYMORE.

MARIAAAAH... HAHA...
YOU TOLD HER TO GO, MARIAH.
YOU TOLD HER TO SAVE HERSELF. TO LOVE ANOTHER.
SHE CHOSE A MAN.
SHE CHOSE TO BE PROPERTY RATHER THAN FACE THE YEARS WITH YOU.
SHE LOVES HIM.
SHE LOVES ONLY HIM.
YOUR CHILD WILL NEVER KNOW HE IS YOUR CHILD.
YOUR SON WILL NEVER KNOW YOUR NAME.

LEAVE. HER. BE.
ENOUGH OF YOUR POISON.
ENOUGH OF YOUR HATE.
A PRETTY SENTIMENT, BUT YOU WILL RATHER HAVE TO BECOME ME TO DESTROY ME, WON'T YOU?
WHO SHALL BE HATED...
...THIS IS THE POWER THAT RULES THE WORLD.

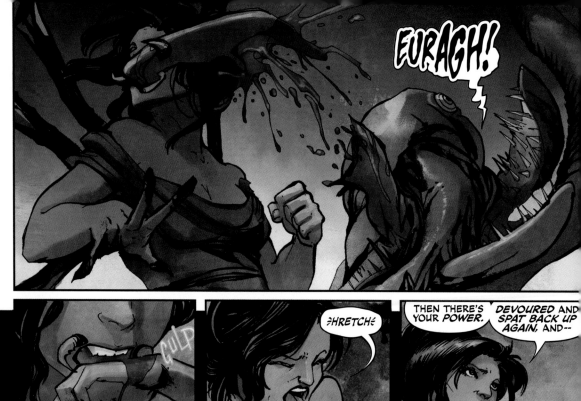

EURAGH!

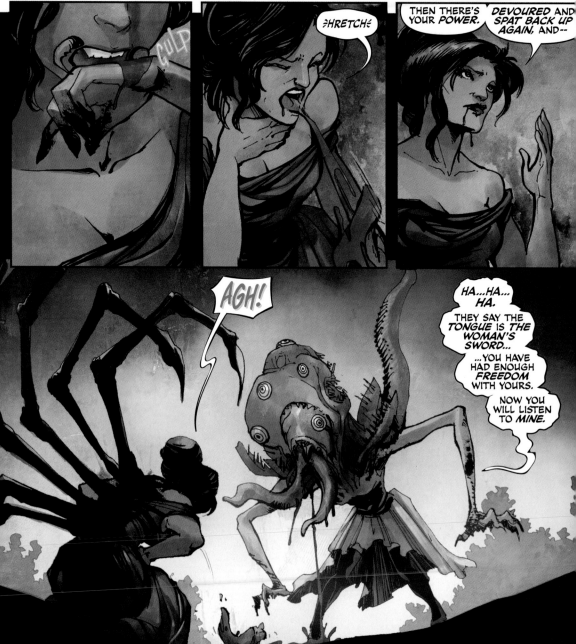

≈GULP≈

≈HRETCH≈

THEN THERE'S YOUR *POWER*.

DEVOURED AND SPAT BACK UP AGAIN, AND--

AGH!

HA...HA... HA.

THEY SAY THE *TONGUE* IS *THE WOMAN'S SWORD*...

...YOU HAVE HAD ENOUGH *FREEDOM* WITH YOURS.

NOW YOU WILL LISTEN TO *MINE*.

ARE YOU *LISTENING,* LADY?
THE ONLY NAME THAT MADE YOU *HAPPY* WAS THE NAME *THEY* GAVE YOU.
LADY... LADY...
...*MY LADY.*

TELL ME, LALITA BERTRAM...
...HOW DO THEY TASTE?
NEXT:
INSEXTS
CHAPTER VII
THE FINAL ACT

"CREEPING THINGS"

7

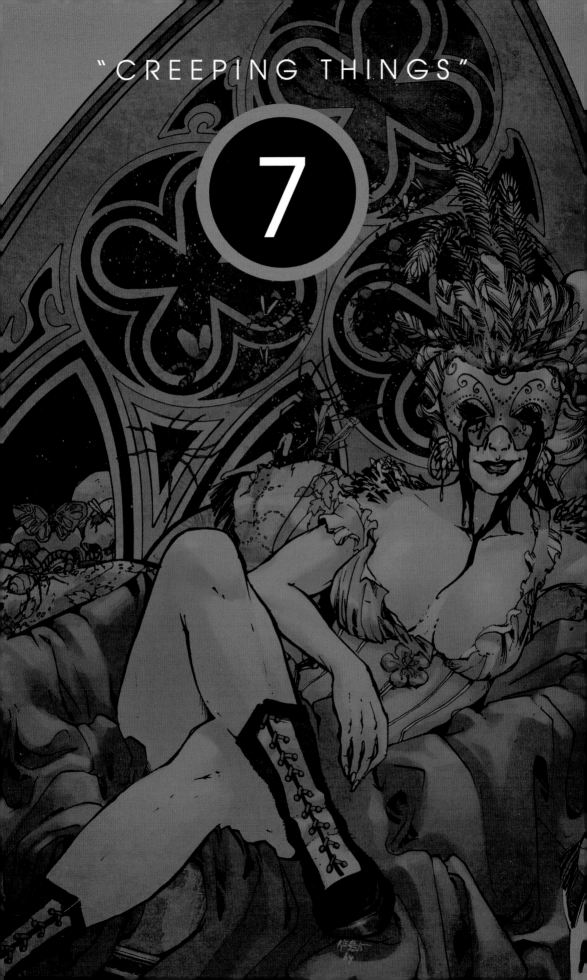

Night. The Brothel
of Madam H.

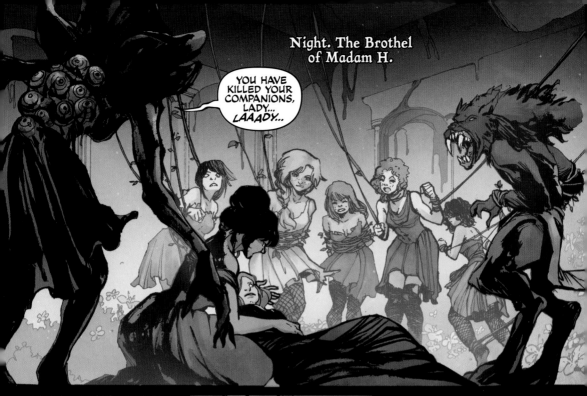

YOU HAVE KILLED YOUR COMPANIONS, LADY... *LAAADY...*

...YOU REACHED, AND WANTED, AND GRASPED FOR THINGS *YOU COULD NOT HOLD...*

...YOU WERE *SPITEFUL, DISSATISFIED, COVETOUS...*

...FOR SUCH IS THE *NATURE* OF *WOMEN.*

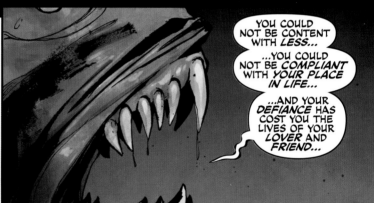

YOU COULD NOT BE CONTENT WITH *LESS...*

...YOU COULD NOT BE *COMPLIANT* WITH *YOUR PLACE IN LIFE...*

...AND YOUR *DEFIANCE* HAS COST YOU THE LIVES OF YOUR *LOVER* AND *FRIEND...*

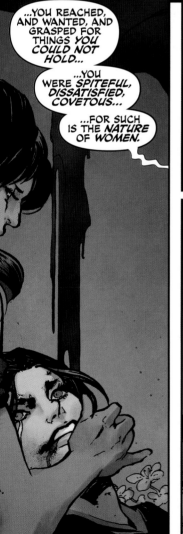

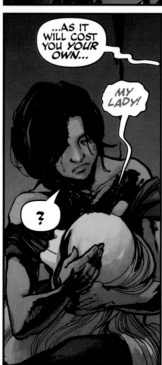

...AS IT WILL COST YOU *YOUR OWN...*

MY LADY!

?

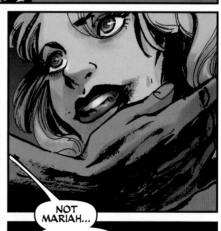

NOT MARIAH...

SYLVIA...?!

SKREEEE
MARIAH!

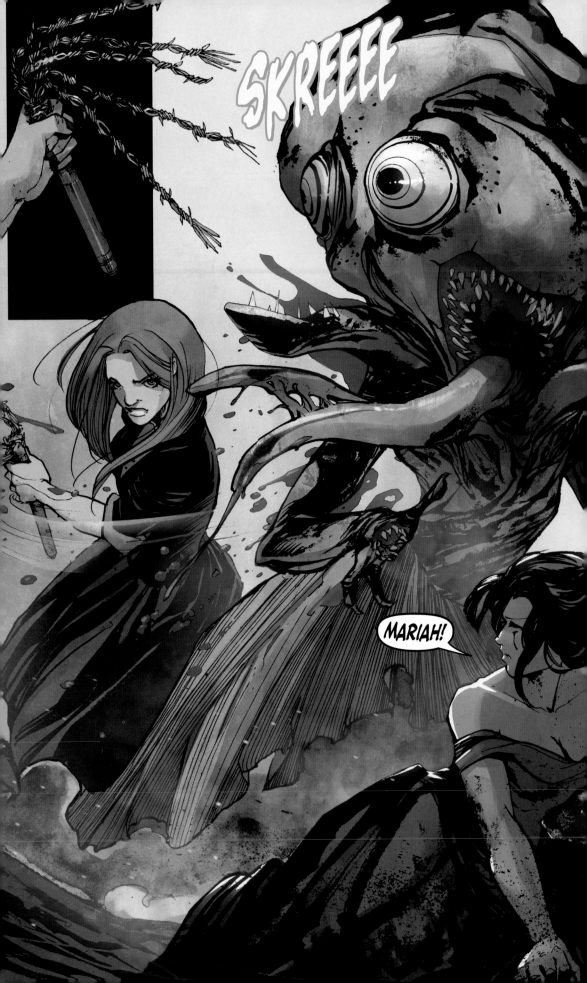

MY LOVE, YOU'RE ALIVE, YOU'RE--
SHHH, MY LADY.
MARIAH, I AM BURNED OUT, BURNED THROUGH, I HAVE NOTHING LEFT! AND IF I DID, I COULD NOT CONTROL IT, COULD NOT--
YOU CAN REST SOON, MY HEART.
MISTRESS HAG, YOU ARE AS KIND TO YOUR SERVANTS AS YOU ARE TO YOUR ENEMIES.
YOU ARE POISON TO ALL THINGS, IN THE END.
TELL ME, DID YOU KILL GEORGE BERTRAM AFTER HE BROUGHT THOSE POOR YOUNG WOMEN TO THIS HOUSE...
...OR AFTER HE STOLE SYLVIA'S CORPSE FROM OUR HOME?
BERTRAM HAD A PURPOSE TO SERVE...
...AS HAVE YOU.
WOMEN ARE FOR SERVING.
WOMEN ARE FOR FUCKING.
WOMEN ARE FOR KILLING.
WOMEN ARE FOR DYING.
!
YOU ARE NOT HEROINES. YOU ARE NOT A GRAND ROMANCE.
YOU ARE AN ABERRATION.
THERE IS ONLY ONE WAY YOUR STORY CAN END--

MY LADY!

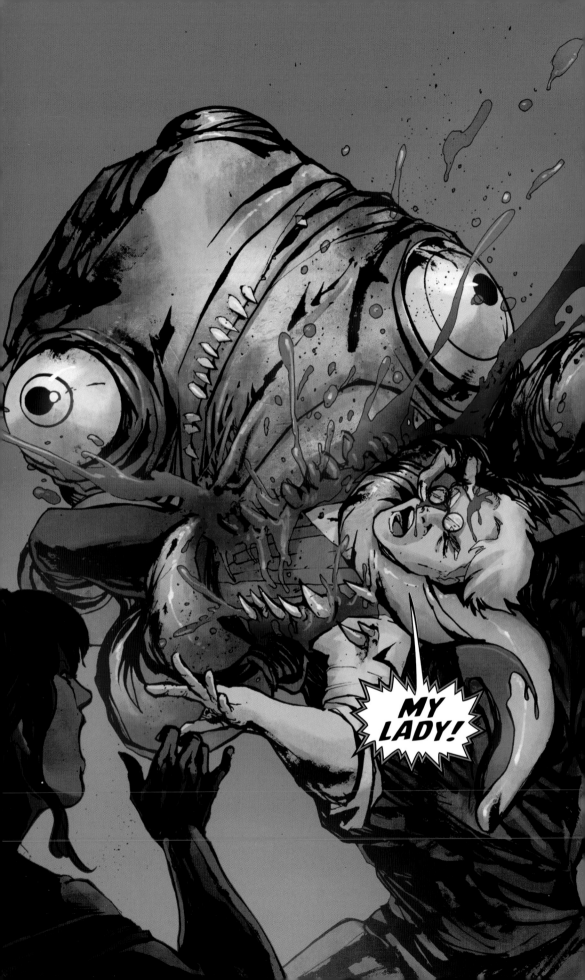

WILLIAM, N-NO--!
YESSSSS, HA HA HA...
HE THOUGHT HE WAS YOUR HERO, DIDN'T HE?
YOUR SAVIOR.
IF HE WAS GOOD ENOUGH, KIND ENOUGH, ONE DAY YOU WOULD TURN TO HIM WITH LOVE IN YOUR EYES...
...BUT HE WASN'T THE HERO OF YOUR STORY.
HE WAS A FOOLISH BOY WHO BELIEVED THAT HE WOULD FIND HIS DAMSEL IN DISTRESS...
...WHO BELIEVED WHITE KNIGHTS COULD NEVER DIE AGAINST DRAGONS.
SAVOR HIS SORROW...
...MY LAAAADY.

AAAAAH!
GET BACK! OH, CHRIST, GET BACK--

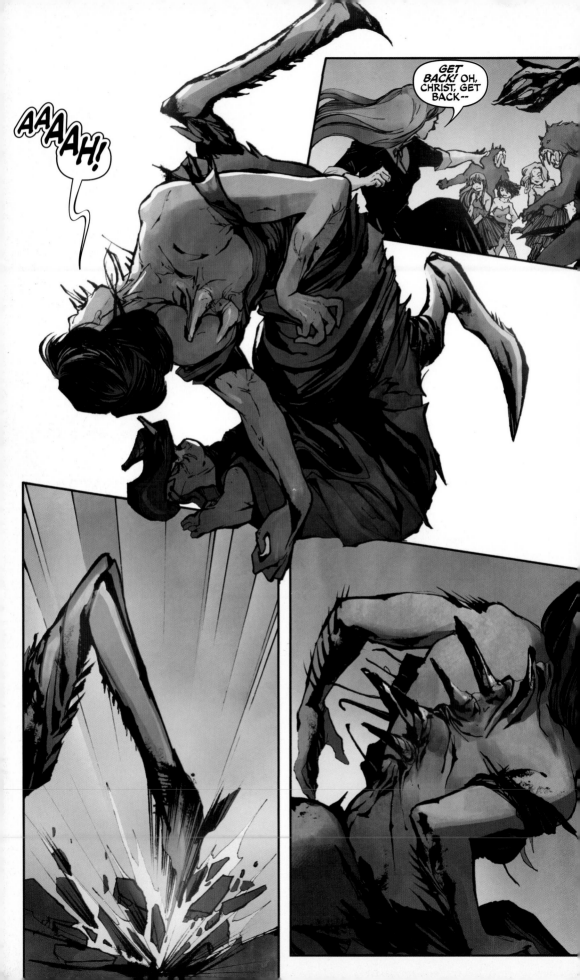

SKREEEEEEEE!

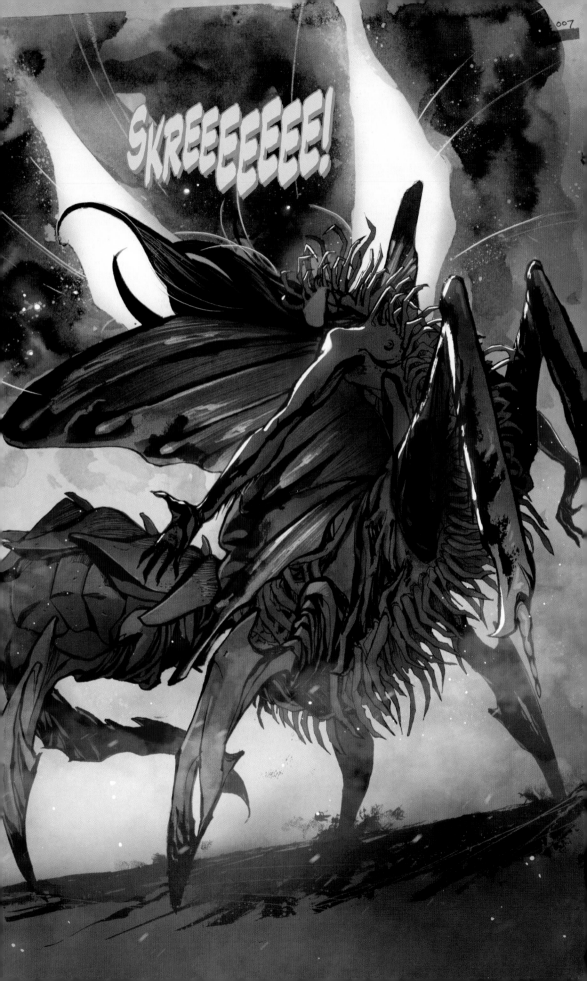

YOU SHALL CLAIM NO MORE OF US.
NOT WOMEN, NOR MEN, NOR LITTLE CHILDREN.
YOU PREY ON THE WEAK AND THE WOUNDED...

...YOU SLITHER IN THROUGH OUR BROKEN HEARTS AND INJURED PRIDE...
...AND YOU MAKE US HATE THE VERY THINGS THAT WE ARE, UNTIL WE ARE YOUR PUPPETS...
...YOU SPOKE OF KNIGHTS AND LADIES AND THOSE WHO DIE AGAINST DRAGONS...
...YOUR HUBRIS WAS THINKING THAT YOU WERE THE DRAGON...
CRACK
...AND THAT THERE WERE NO BETTER MONSTERS...

...TO BRING YOU DOWN.

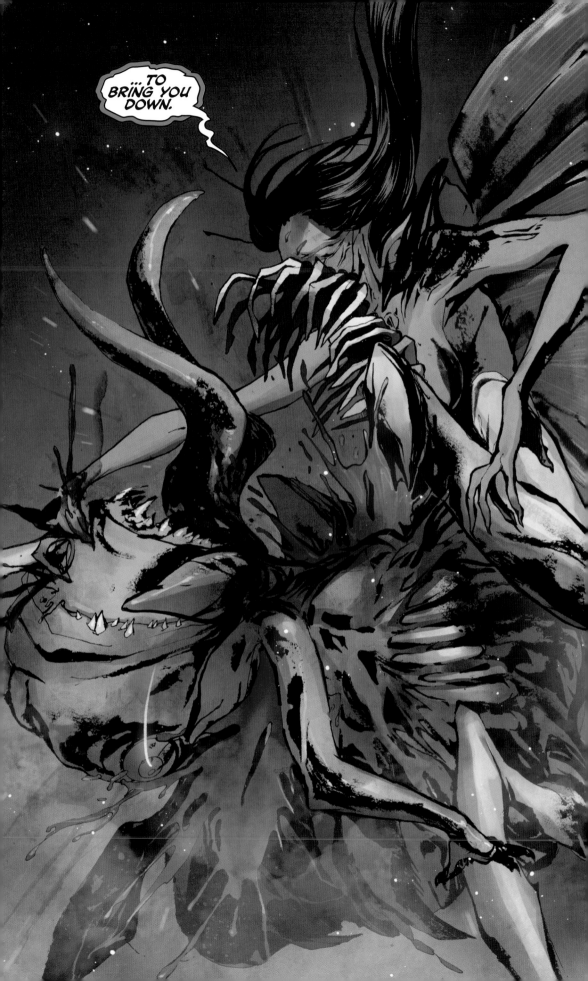

STAY BACK, BROTHERS! STAY BACK FROM THE BEAST!
MY LADY!
KILL THEM, WHILE THE FIENDS ARE STILL WEAK!
KILL THE MONSTRESS, FOR SHE WILL BECOME THE NEW HAG.
KILL THE WITCH-WOMAN, WHO IS HER KEEPER.
KILL THE WHORES, FOR THEY WERE THE SERVANTS OF SIN.
B-BROTHER ASHER!
BROTHER ASHER...
...IF THESE ARE YOUR ORDERS...

...YOU WERE MORE A SERVANT OF THE HAG...
"...THAN YOU WERE EVER A SERVANT OF THE LORD!"

THE HOUSE... THE HOUSE IS CRUMBLING...
IT WAS ONLY THE HAG'S GLAMOUR THAT MADE IT SEEM SO RICH...
AT LEAST...AT FIRST.
ROT AND GRIME... THAT'S ALL IT EVER WAS.
THAT'S ALL SHE EVER WAS.
A HATE, MADE FLESH...
A HATRED OF WOMEN.
KK-KRNCH
ELSIE?
OH, GOD, DID THE HAG HAVE YOU LOCKED UP ALL THAT TIME, CHILD?
LEVERAGE, AGAINST BERTRAM? ONE FINAL GAMBIT?
HERE, CHILD, IS IT TIME--?
SHE MUST BE GOTTEN TO A DOCTOR!
A...A DOCTOR... WILLIAM...
...
I WILL LIVE.
GO, MY LOVE.
"THE DEAD WILL WAIT.
"THE LIVING WILL LEARN.
"BUT NEW LIFE...NEW JOY TO COME..."

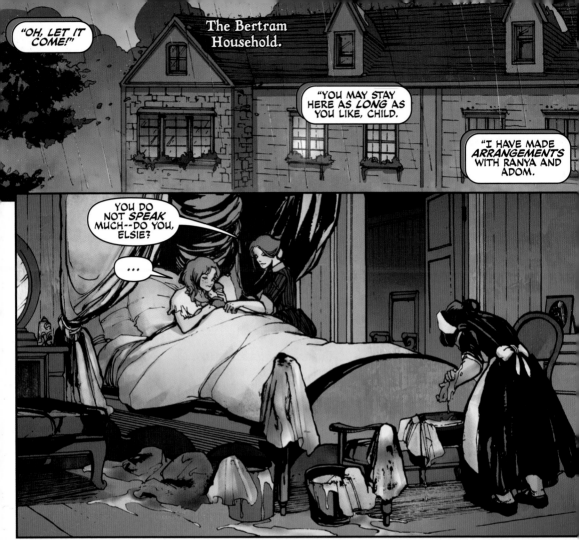

"OH, LET IT COME!"

The Bertram Household.

"YOU MAY STAY HERE AS *LONG* AS YOU LIKE, CHILD.

"I HAVE MADE *ARRANGEMENTS* WITH RANYA AND ADOM.

YOU DO NOT *SPEAK* MUCH--DO YOU, ELSIE?

...

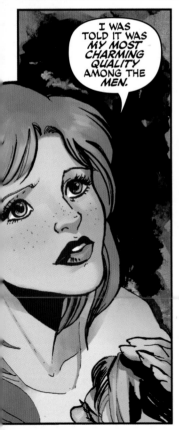

I WAS TOLD IT WAS *MY MOST CHARMING QUALITY* AMONG THE MEN.

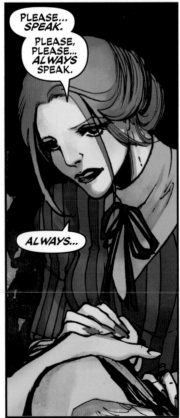

PLEASE... *SPEAK.*

PLEASE, PLEASE... *ALWAYS* SPEAK.

ALWAYS...

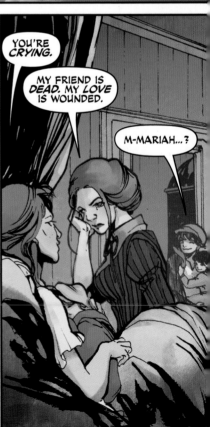

YOU'RE *CRYING.*

MY FRIEND IS *DEAD.* MY *LOVE* IS WOUNDED.

M-MARIAH...?

DID YOU THINK FREEDOM AND LOVE WOULD COME WITHOUT PRICE?
DID YOU THINK YOU COULD EXIST IN THIS WORLD WITHOUT IT PUNISHING YOU FOR THAT EXISTENCE?
I DIDN'T THINK THE PRICE WOULD BE SO HIGH.
THE WORLD WILL ALWAYS COME FOR US.
THE WORLD WILL ALWAYS WANT US TO SUFFER.
WE ARE THE PROOF THAT A ROTTING WORLD STILL HAS POWER OVER SOMETHING, AND WHO HOLDS POWER IS THE ONLY RULE THERE HAS EVER BEEN.
DEFY IT.
HOW?
SPEAK.
SING.
AND TRY TO FIND A WAY...

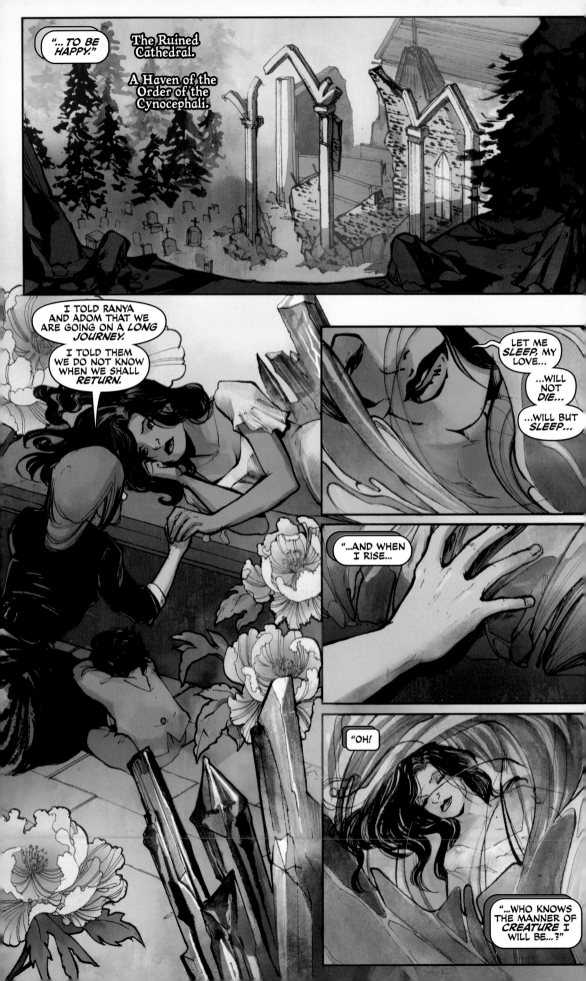

"...TO BE HAPPY."

The Ruined Cathedral.

A Haven of the Order of the Cynocephali.

I TOLD RANYA AND ADOM THAT WE ARE GOING ON A *LONG JOURNEY.*

I TOLD THEM WE DO NOT KNOW WHEN WE SHALL *RETURN.*

LET ME *SLEEP,* MY LOVE...

...WILL NOT *DIE...*

...WILL BUT *SLEEP...*

"...AND WHEN I RISE...

"OH!

"...WHO KNOWS THE MANNER OF *CREATURE* I WILL BE...?"

TELL ME...
...WHAT IS TO BECOME OF US?
WE HAVE NOTHING.
THE HAG TOOK OUR HOME FROM US, TOOK OUR HEARTS FROM US, BURNED OUT WHAT COULD STILL FEEL JOY INSIDE OF US.
WHAT YOU DO NOW...
...
...IS WHATEVER YOU CHOOSE TO DO.
PERHAPS YOU WILL HEAL. PERHAPS YOU WILL ALWAYS HURT.
BUT YOU LIVE... AND WHILE YOU LIVE, AS LONG AS YOU LIVE, YOU MAY CHOOSE WHAT TO DO.
FIND A HOUSE OF YOUR OWN...
...GO INTO THE WORLD...
OR COME WITH US, FOR THERE ARE MANY MORE MONSTERS TO HUNT.
WILL YOU... WILL YOU FIRST HELP ME BURY WILLIAM?
AYE, MY LADY.
I AM NOT A LADY.
YES, YOU ARE.
YOU'RE OUR LADY.
OUR LADIES... OF EVERY CREEPING THING...

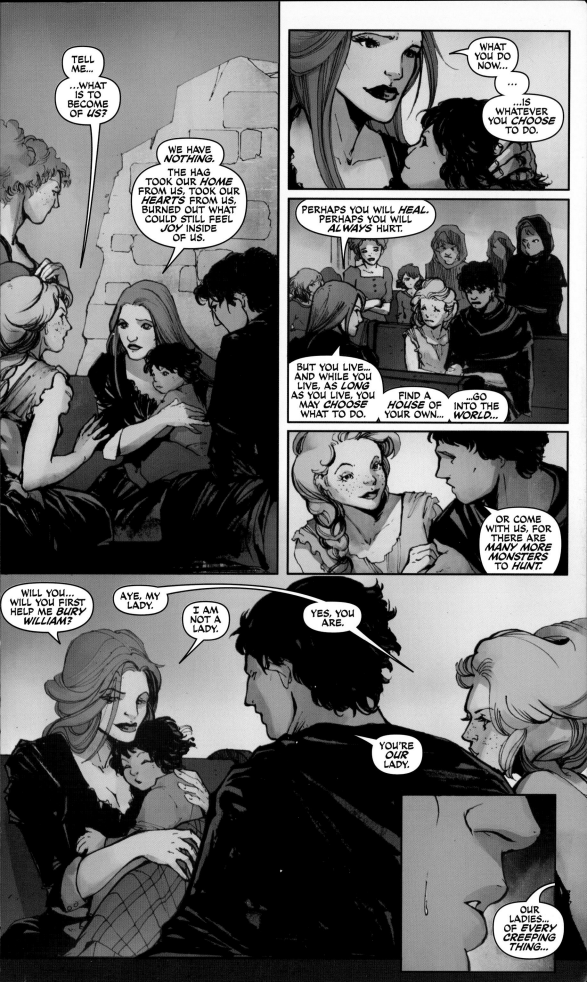

Dawn.
I WASN'T KNOWING WILLIAM WELL.
I WASN'T EVEN KNOWIN' HIS TRUE NAME *WAS* WILLIAM.
BUT HE WAS *KIND.* AND HE TRIED TO *PROTECT US.*
"AND I THINK HE WAS A *GOOD MAN.*"
REQUIES
DR. WILLIAM
DR. WILLIAM TAYLOR
WE MIGHT'VE BEEN *HAPPY,* THE THREE OF US.
THE *FOUR* OF US...
...ONE *HAPPY FAMILY.*
AND PERHAPS WE MAY BE HAPPY *YET,* MY WILL...
...*OUR* WILL.
"YES.
"*THAT* IS WHAT WE FOUND."

WAS IT WORTH IT?
OF COURSE IT WAS.
SPEAK...
...SING...
...AND TRY TO BE *HAPPY.*
♪♬ FROM ROT THE BEAUTIES OF THE WORLD CAN ONLY EVER SPRING ♬♪
♪♬ FROM MISERY AND SORROW COMES THE MUSIC THAT WE SING ♬♪
♬♪ THE SWEETEST SUMMER ROSES ARISE FROM SQUELCHING MUD ♪♬
♪♬ AND WE WHO LIVE TO SUFFER AS SEASONS FLAME AND DIE ♬♪
♪♬ KNOW THE HOPE OF EVERY CREEPING THING... ♪♬

♪♬... TO BE A BUTTERFLY.♪♬
END OF ARC ONE.
INSEXTS

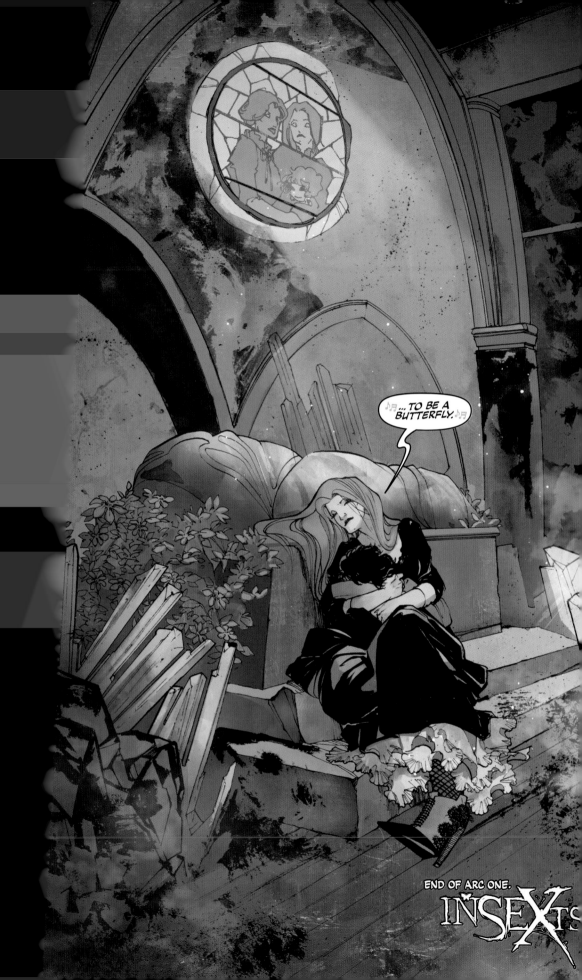

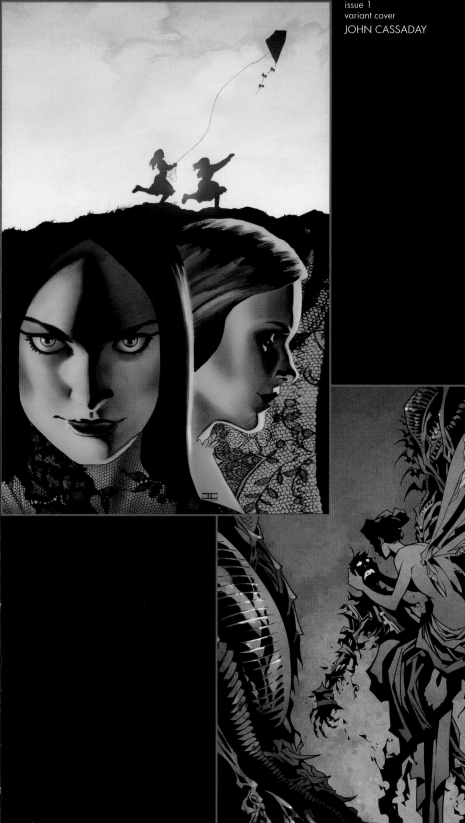

issue 1
variant cover
JOHN CASSADAY

issue 1
variant cover
PHIL HESTER

MARGUERITE BENNETT writer
🐦 @EvilMarguerite

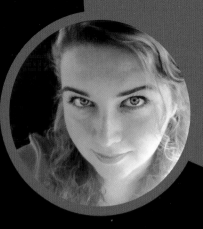

Marguerite Bennett is a comic book writer from Richmond, Virginia, who currently splits her time between Los Angeles and New York City. She received her MFA in Creative Writing from Sarah Lawrence College in 2013 and quickly went on to work for DC Comics, Marvel, BOOM! Studios, Dynamite, and IDW on projects ranging from *Batman*, *Bombshells*, and *A-Force* to *Angela: Asgard's Assassin*, *Red Sonja*, and FOX TV's *Sleepy Hollow*. INSEXTS is her first creator-owned work.

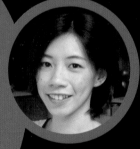

ARIELA KRISTANTINA artist
🐦 @ARIELAkris

Ariela is a comic artist from Jakarta, Indonesia. She's now pursuing her comics career in America. Ariela was involved in several anthologies before she got her first big break in 2014 as the artist for *The Logan Legacy* #2 at Marvel. Her other works for Marvel include several issues of *Wolverines* as well as being a contributor on *Wolverine and The X-Men* #6. She's also working for BOOM! Studios with Justin Jordan for *Deep State* (#1-#8) and for Dark Horse with Brian Wood for *Rebels* #8.

BRYAN VALENZA colorist
🐦 @Bryanvalenza

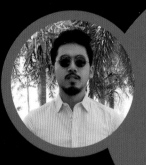

Born and raised in Jakarta, Indonesia, Bryan studied Visual Communication Design at Institut Teknologi Nasional in 2010. He scored his first comic book gig in 2011. Some of his coloring projects include *Cain: First Born* #1-5, *Hit List* #1-5 from Zenescope, *Inferno: Age of Darkness*, *Inferno: Rings of Hell*, and *Skies of Fire*.

JESSICA KHOLINNE colorist
🐦 @jessicakholinne

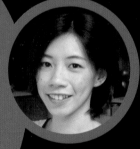

Jessica Kholinne is an Indonesian colorist who grew up loving comic books, movies and games. She has worked for several major publishers over the past few years with projects that include *X-Treme X-Men*, *Voodoo*, *Code Monkey Save World* and now INSEXTS with AfterShock Comics.

A LARGER WORLD letterers
🐦 @A_Larger_World

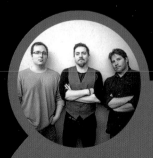

Troy Peteri, Dave Lanphear and Joshua Cozine are collectively known as A Larger World Studios. They've lettered everything from *The Avengers*, *Iron Man*, *Wolverine*, *Amazing Spider-Man* and *X-Men* to more recent titles like *The Spirit*, *Batman & Robin Eternal* and *Pacific Rim*. They can be reached at studio@largerworld.com for your lettering and design needs.